THIS BOOK
BELONGS TO:

Montana ☺

Cavarra ☺

The Child's Christmas

CHARLES ROBINSON

CHILDREN'S CLASSICS

This unique series of Children's Classics™ features accessible and highly readable texts paired with the work of talented and brilliant illustrators of bygone days to create fine editions for today's parents and children to rediscover and treasure. Besides being a handsome addition to any home library, this series features genuine bonded-leather spines stamped in gold, full-color illustrations, and high-quality acid-free paper that will enable these books to be passed from one generation to the next.

The Child's Christmas

PICTURED BY CHARLES ROBINSON

WITH TEXT BY EVELYN SHARP

CHILDREN'S CLASSICS

NEW YORK

This 1991 edition is published by Children's Classics,
a division of dilithium Press, Ltd., distributed by Outlet Book Company, Inc.,
a Random House Company, 225 Park Avenue South,
New York, New York 10003.

DILITHIUM is a registered trademark
and CHILDREN'S CLASSICS is a trademark of dilithium Press, Ltd.

Printed and bound in the United States of America

For this edition of The Child's Christmas:

Cover design: Clair Moritz
Interior design: Helene Berinsky
Production supervision: Susan Wein

Library of Congress Cataloging-in-Publication Data

Sharp, Evelyn, 1869–1955.
The child's Christmas / with text by Evelyn Sharp ; pictured by
Charles Robinson.
p.   cm.
Summary: Members of an English country family experience the
excitement and beauty of an old-fashioned Christmas season, in
events leading from the early days of decoration and preparation
through New Year's Day and up to Twelfth Night.
ISBN 0–517–03369–0
[1. Christmas—Fiction.   2. England—Fiction.]   I. Robinson,
Charles, ill.   II. Title.
PZ7.S531Ci   1991   91–19813
[Fic]—dc20   CIP
                                                      AC

8   7   6   5   4   3   2   1

To Christmas Day
Babies
and
Other
Day
Babies
All the
World
over

Contents

COLOR ILLUSTRATIONS 🍃 🍃 🍃

PREFACE TO THIS EDITION

CHARLES ROBINSON, one of the most gifted and prolific book illustrators in Edwardian England, endowed this Christmas treasure trove with artistry in three different forms: beautiful color plates portraying the traditional events of Christmas, striking full-page images in black and white of the typical joys of the season, and delightful line drawings throughout the text, which humorously and affectionately capture intimate scenes of family life.

Charles Robinson was born into an artistic family—he was the son of a wood engraver and his brothers, William Heath Robinson and Thomas Heath Robinson, were also artists and illustrators. But the achievements of Charles were outstanding: he illustrated well over one hundred books, mostly for children, among them, Robert Louis Stevenson's *A Child's Garden of Verses* and *Aesop's Fables*. His love of gardens was particularly strong, and was movingly represented in works such as *The Secret Garden*, by Frances Hodgson Burnett.

This edition represents the first time that Charles Robinson's art has been featured in this series. Children's Classics are pleased and proud to present this distinguished and multitalented artist to today's readers.

CLAIRE BOOSS
Series Editor

1991

Note: The publishers would like to express their appreciation to Lucille Santarelli, who first suggested the inclusion of this book in the Children's Classics series.

FOREWORD

THE CHILD'S CHRISTMAS gives us what we most need—a guidebook to the way Christmas used to be. It gives us the opportunity to witness some of the wonderful customs and traditions that the British still retain. It is, in a sense, a "how-to" book, so that we can again make Christmastime what it once was, even if we don't live in Victorian England. Forget that the extended family is fast becoming obsolete, that in many families both parents work, and that some are single-parent households. Forget all the realities that make our Christmas a long, commercial build-up to one shining day—followed by a big letdown.

The best things about this book (and there are so many wonderful ones that it is difficult to list them all) are that they show us all the events, large and small, of an "old-fashioned" Christmas, in charming and succinct detail. Each chapter is no longer than a page or two—the perfect length for a bedtime story beginning after Thanksgiving and continuing until the middle of January, when the Christmas season really ends.

Taking an English country family as its focal point and the children in the family as the core, Evelyn Sharp leads us deftly and lovingly through the days of preparation, the wondrous eve, the day itself, the days afterward—Boxing Day, New Year's Eve, New Year's Day, Twelfth Night—and helps us to understand and experience Christmastime as the most beautiful and exciting period of the year.

This is not a book about religious observance. It is, rather, a historical diary which manages to include the best of everything about the season that children like most. And the child in each of us cannot fail to respond to this invitation to wonder.

Of course, everything is perfect. The snow falls just at the right time; the world is transformed into a fairyland. The cost of living has not yet escalated to a point where it is unthinkable for children to send Christmas cards by mail. (In the book the cost of mailing a card is a penny a piece, and the children save all year for this.) The postman works on Christmas Day to deliver the cards and presents that were mailed on Christmas Eve. The house is large enough to accommodate all the grandparents and cousins who come to visit for the entire holiday season, and there is a nanny to relieve Mother and Father of the troubles of getting impatient toddlers and youngsters off to bed. There are also charmingly unfamiliar customs. Not only the carolers come by to sing on Christmas Eve, but a group of musicians called "the waits" fill the hours before midnight with enchanting seasonal music as they stroll the streets of the town with their instruments. The stillness of the snow-covered streets makes the out-of-doors a huge but intimate hall for these players, and the children in their beds fall asleep listening to the hushed and delicate notes. But above all, Santa Claus really does exist. His home is carefully described, his reindeer, his sleigh, his trip, and his decisions about gifts for children who have not been altogether good (but not altogether bad, either). He is never seen by the children (that would be too much), but he does everything one would want of him without overdoing it.

Christmas Day itself is an orchestrated masterpiece. It begins with the opening of the gifts, followed by the trip to church, and then the journey homeward for the Christmas dinner. To give you a taste of what is involved, here are the little chapters on the dinner alone:

> GRANDPAPA'S SPEECH
> THE MINCE PIES
> THE DOG'S CHRISTMAS DINNER
> THE CAT'S CHRISTMAS DINNER
> THE ROBIN'S CHRISTMAS DINNER
> GRANDPAPA'S YOUNG DAYS
> THE DESSERT
> GRANDPAPA'S SONG
> AFTER DESSERT

"The Dessert" is a delightful description of that time following the big dinner when a giddy drowsiness creeps in.

> Father could do lovely things with the dessert. He could play the battle of Trafalgar in a finger bowl with nut shells. He could make an orange into an old man with a row of giant's teeth and a horrible grin. . . . That pleased Grandmamma, and she showed the little girls how to make a raisin into a tea-pot, with a stalk for a handle and an almond for a spout. . . . Then Pat took out his new knife and said he was going to turn a candied apricot into an old man . . .

The same attention to an unwritten schedule is given to the after-dinner phase of the day, with a little chapter devoted to each separate event, from roasting chestnuts, through lighting candles, games, songs, recitations, piano performances by the youngsters, and dances, to the final hours of the children's day. This is a children's book and we are not, therefore given a description of the adults' activities following the children's bedtime, which are of no importance.

And now the book becomes an arresting and wonderful surprise. The days after Christmas—which, for most modern American families, are filled with nothing more interesting than returning presents, parents going back to work, children getting bored with new toys—for our storybook children, are as full of fun and excitement, anticipation and preparation, as the days before Christmas. Boxing Day, which remains a standard practice in Great Britain today, is the day after Christmas when all the people who help to make life run smoothly are remembered. The postman, the butcher, the bell-ringers of the church, all receive boxes of either pennies or gifts. Preparing the boxes and giving them is as exciting to the children as preparing Christmas presents for each other.

Of course, there is the Christmas party: invitations, preparations, the games (eight of them in all, and each one with its very own little chapter). I can just hear the young children whose parents have read the chapter to them the night before saying, "Let's play Oranges and Lemons" (a kind of tug-of-war.) Then there is the Christmas panto-mime, a play which the children are taken to each year, then the resolutions for the New Year, the Twelfth Night cake, the January thaw, and finally, the end of the season, when cousins and grandparents bundle into their cars and take their leave.

Christmastime has truly been a month of Sundays for the child. A month of special events, repeated each year; but each year retaining the magical beauty and perhaps growing a little brighter, a little better, as the child grows from babyhood to eight or nine: these are the years of *The Child's Christmas*. And if a wise parent shares this marvelous book with his or her children as a tradition during those years or tries in his or her own special way to adapt some of the customs of the Victorian period, there is little doubt that today's child can experience the thrill of the perfect Christmas, if only in storyland. The sharing of these little chapters by parent and child can bring the vanishing warmth and wonder into each home and inspire a youngster to try to achieve some of that warmth and wonder in his or her own life.

PATRICIA BARRETT PERKINS

Baltimore, Maryland
1991

EDITORIAL NOTE

The modern reader may be surprised to discover certain old-fashioned styles of punctuation and spelling, but these have been retained in order to convey the flavor of the original edition. However, some words and phrases that may be unfamiliar to the reader have been defined in footnotes to the text.

The Child's Christmas

CHARLES ROBINSON

STIRRING THE CHRISTMAS PUDDING

Waiting for Christmas

DOWNSTAIRS in the kitchen the Christmas pudding was being stirred. Upstairs in the nursery, Nancy stood on a chair and counted off the days on the calendar, one by one, with her short fat finger.

"Look, Sophia!" she said to her best doll, who sat exhausted on the arm of the chair, after a very tiring morning of being dressed and washed by her mistress. "Only one more day to Christmas Eve! Oh, Sophia, do look glad!"

Sophia did not, however, alter her expression, not even when Nancy seized her by one arm and dragged her off to stir the pudding. Elfie lingered behind and looked out of the window. "Do you think the snow fairies will come before Christmas Day, Nurse?" she asked.

"You come and stir the pudding, Miss Elfie, and we'll see," said Nurse, who did not think much of fairies.

Elfie pressed her face flat against the window pane, and whispered: "Father Christmas, please bring the snow fairies." Then away she scampered to stir the pudding too.

Everybody stirred the pudding, Father and Mother and Pat and Nancy and Nurse and Baby; and Baby nearly fell into it. "Nasty pudding!" he said, when Cook gave him some of it on her finger to taste.

Outside in the garden, Father Christmas was lifting his cloak and shaking the snow fairies out of it as fast as he could.

"We shall have an old-fashioned Christmas after all!" said Mother, when she saw the snow.

"Thank you, Father Christmas!" cried little Elfie.

Putting up Decorations

OLD PETER, the gardener, was up before breakfast on Christmas Eve, cutting evergreens. Pat was up before breakfast too, nearly ten minutes before; and he helped Peter. He was not much help, for there was only one blade in his knife and that was broken; still, he felt important. After breakfast, everybody came and put up the decorations. The Squire* stood at the top of a ladder and put up wreaths. Mother made wreaths for him to put up. Nurse kept Baby from pricking himself. Nancy made pretty paper chains for

* "Squire" is the title given to the owner of a country estate, the Father in this family.

Pat to hang across the old hall, and her dolly lay on the floor and stared up at the ceiling. So everybody was busy.

CHARLES ROBINSON.

The great branches that Peter brought in from the garden were white with snow. "I wish the snow would not melt," said Mother; "snow is so pretty."

"Snow is wet," said Father, and he shook the branches. Elfie held out her pinafore to catch the snow fairies as they came tumbling down; but when she looked she found nothing but drops of water. "I suppose they have flown away," she said.

"I like snow," said Baby, sucking the wet leaves when Nurse was not looking. Baby was busy too.

Sophia did not like snow, though she said nothing when Pat dropped some in her mouth.

"You are very unkind to her, Pat," said Nancy, picking up her dolly, and shaking out the snow.

BUYING PRESENTS

THERE was a clatter on the nursery floor, and three empty money-boxes stood beside three heaps of pennies. Nancy's was the biggest heap, and Elfie's was the second biggest, and Pat's was the smallest.

"I do wish I had not spent so much money on toffee, last week," sighed Pat.

"That comes of being greedy," said Nurse, who never lost an opportunity of this sort. "Now, make haste and get ready, or we shall not finish our shopping before dinner-time."

Then Baby, who had no money-box, was given a penny to hold, and the whole family set out for the town to buy presents. Father and Mother came too, so when they were all inside the first shop there was scarcely room to move. But the shopman did not seem to mind.

"The more the merrier," he said; and Elfie wondered why

people always said that, when there was such a crowd that she could not see anything but legs and elbows. Then the shopman lifted her on to a chair, and they all began to choose Christmas cards. It was very exciting, because, of course, nobody wanted anybody else to see what cards were being

bought, and it was not easy in such a small shop to buy them in private. Still, the shopman was very obliging, and that was a great help.

Then they all came out of that shop and went on to the most important shop in the town, which, of course, was a toy-shop. It was covered all over with toys; they hung from

[8]

the roof and they lay about the floor; it was quite difficult to walk without stepping on them.

"Which toy do you like best, Baby?" asked Mother.

"I like them all best," said Baby. But when Nurse explained that at Christmas time people bought toys for other people, he held out a hot penny and said: "A present for Nancy, please."

At Christmas time, presents have to be bought in a whisper. The toy-shop woman did all the

selling in a whisper, too; so nobody knew what was in anybody else's parcel. But everybody had hopes, especially Father.

"I do hope somebody bought me a pretty doll," he said. "Do you think anybody did, Elfie?"

"P'r'aps," said Elfie; and she held on tight to her parcel with both hands.

Father still hoped.

THE CAROL SINGERS

JUST as everybody was getting ready for dinner, the sound of children's voices came up from the garden below. In a moment, combs and brushes and sponges were flung on one side, and down they all scampered to the front door to welcome the carol singers. There they stood on the gravel path outside, a row of rosy-cheeked boys and girls, singing away as only girls and boys can sing when the sun shines, and the snow glistens, and it is going to be Christmas Day tomorrow. When they had sung all the carols they knew,

the children made them come indoors; and Mother gave them as much ginger - beer and plum-cake as they wanted. And then Father gave them each a bright sixpence, and they went away, wishing it was Christmas all the year round.

"I'd like to be a carol singer," sighed Pat, thinking of his empty money-box.

"Ah," said Father, "you would not like to be a carol singer if you lived in town instead of in the country. In London, the carol singers are not rosy-cheeked; they are poor and hungry, with pale faces and thin cheeks, and they go round singing at other people's doors till late at night, and very often nobody gives them any money or anything nice to eat."

"I don't want to be a carol singer," Pat said, then.

But they all wished, like the country carol singers, that it was Christmas all the year round.

ADDRESSING THE CARDS

THERE is a great deal to do on Christmas Eve in the afternoon. For one thing, there are all the cards to be addressed, and this cannot be done without a great deal of patience and a great deal of ink. Baby used up more ink than anybody; though he did not know how to write. But Nancy held his hand and guided it over his Christmas card so that he wrote in big shaky letters—"To Mother from Baby." Then he felt very proud of himself, and put his finger in the ink-pot and sucked it to see if the black would come off. It did come off, and the taste was very nasty. "I don't like writing," said Baby, as Nurse carried him off to be washed.

Elfie could not write, either; but she knew how to print capital letters, so she printed the words as Nancy spelt them to her.   Unfortunately, Nancy forgot to tell her where the words ended, so when the card was addressed it looked like this—

TOMOTHERFROMELFIE

But mothers always understand that kind of writing; so it did not matter.

Pat knew how to write, so he addressed his cards by himself.   He shook the whole table when he wrote.   He curled one leg tightly round his chair, and with the other he kicked everybody within reach.   He wrote with his mouth wide open and his nose very close to the envelope, and a good deal of the ink went on to his face by mistake.   He would not let Nancy help him because he knew how to write, and when he had finished, this is what he had written—

to mother. wishing her a merry Christmass.

"I am glad we do not have cards to address every day," said Nancy, when she at last had a moment's peace in which to address her own.

"It is quite easy when you know how," said Pat in a superior tone.

AT THE POST OFFICE

NOW, we must go and post our letters," said Nancy, who, being the eldest, always arranged these things. "It will not be a proper surprise for Mother unless her cards come by post."

"It's a great waste of a penny stamp," said Nurse. But she did not raise any more objections as it was Christmas Eve, and she took them all down to the post-office.

COMING OUT OF THE POST OFFICE

Anybody could have guessed from the look of the post-office what time of year it was. Outside in the snow stood the postman with the large barrow he had just wheeled up from the station, all full to overflowing with brown paper parcels. There were round parcels and square parcels, big parcels and little parcels, hard parcels with corners, and soft squashy parcels. The wheel-barrow was never so full as that at any other time of the year.

Inside the post-office were rows and rows of people with parcels in their hands. The post-office people were dreadfully busy, but they found time to wish everyone a happy Christmas, even Baby; and they did not grumble once when they had to stop weighing parcels and give the children a penny stamp each. It is not easy to grumble on Christmas Eve, even if you are somebody in a post-office.

"If people go on sending parcels like this, there will be nothing left for Santa Claus to do," said Elfie.

"P'r'aps they send them to Santa Claus first, and then he brings them to us," said Nancy. "Do you think so, Nurse?"

"There's no knowing what will happen if you are good children," said Nurse.

"I wonder how good we've got to be," said Pat, anxiously.

THE CARRIER

T the back door stood the carrier's cart. It was stuffed full of hampers, and it was decorated with bits of holly, and it looked as if it were saying "A Merry Christmas" at the top of its voice. And that is just what old Jacob did say when he saw the children.

"Are all the hampers for us, Jacob?" cried Pat.

Jacob shook his head. Only three of the hampers were for them; but they were three of the heaviest.

"One from Grandpapa, and one from Uncle Jim, and one from Great-Aunt Maria," said Nancy, reading the labels. "Grandpapa's will be lovely, and so will Uncle Jim's; but I am not sure about Great-Aunt Maria's."

"Hers will be full of useful presents," sighed Pat.

"Good children take what is given them and are grateful," said Nurse.

"It is very difficult to be grateful for Great-Aunt Maria's presents," said Pat.

At this moment Baby tried to pull one of the hampers out of the cart. "I want all the hampers," he shouted. "I like hampers."

CHARLES ROBINSON

"It is greedy to want other people's hampers," said Nurse. This did not, however, make Baby change his mind about hampers.

The carrier did not go away when he had taken the hampers into the house. He looked again inside the cart.

"Is there another hamper?" asked Pat, feeling excited.

"Not exactly what you might call a hamper, Master Pat," said Jacob.

"Did the fairies send it, Jacob?" asked Elfie, eagerly.

"That they didn't,

missy," chuckled old Jacob. "It was Farmer Hobson's wife as sent it, and what she'll say if I've mislaid it——"

"I hope you haven't mislaid it," said Pat, anxiously.

"I know what it is!" cried Nancy. "It's the turkey!"

And so it was; for at that moment old Jacob gave a tug and pulled it out of the cart.

"Nice dicky bird," said Baby. "Pretty red cheeks."

Then Cook came and carried off the turkey to the larder and the carrier cracked his whip and drove off.

"I want all the hampers," said Baby. "Why has he taken them away?"

Nancy and Pat and Elfie wanted the other hampers, too. But, of course, they were far too grown-up to mention this.

"A hamper in the hand is worth two in the bush," said Nurse, trying to console Baby.

"What bush?" asked Baby, looking about him, eagerly. "I can't see any hampers in the bushes."

THE YULE LOG

THE Squire liked old customs, as all nice people do; so he asked Tommy, the garden boy, if the Yule log was ready, and all the children, except Baby, helped him to pull it into the house.

"There is plenty of wood indoors," said Nancy. "Why are we taking in this enormous big log?"

"Everybody who helps to pull in the Yule log will be lucky all the year," explained Father. After that, Nurse and Baby came and pulled too; and so the great log was brought into the hall and laid on the big open hearth, ready to be lighted in the evening. For the Yule log is always lighted on Christmas Eve, and it keeps burning all through Christmas week.

PACKING HAMPERS

N OW," said Mother, "come and pack hampers for the village people, so that they may have a happy Christmas, too. What shall we put into Mrs. Wilson's hamper?"

"I think she would like a knife with two blades and a cork-screw," said Pat.

Mother did not, however, agree with Pat; so they packed the hamper with a warm shawl and a plum-pudding and a goose. "It looks like one of Great-Aunt Maria's useful hampers," said Pat.

"Now," said Mother, "there is old Jo Brown. What shall he have?"

"I think," said Elfie, "that he would like a dolly with curly hair and blue eyes." But Mother did not agree with Elfie, either; so they packed that hamper with snuff and tobacco and beef and boots. "He will be very glad that Christmas comes but once a year," thought Elfie.

Just as they packed the last hamper, there was a sort of a puffing and a snorting and a rushing and a grunting, outside the front door. There was a loud horn too, that

kept on hooting all the while; so it was quite easy to guess where the noise came from.

Then everybody became most excited.

"Here are the cousins!" cried Mother.

"And Grandpapa and Grandmamma!" cried the girls.

"I'll be there first," said Pat, taking a flying leap over the last hamper.

"I am firstest," said Baby, as he sat down on the door mat.

THE CHRISTMAS GUESTS

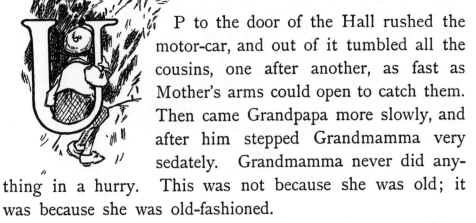

U P to the door of the Hall rushed the motor-car, and out of it tumbled all the cousins, one after another, as fast as Mother's arms could open to catch them. Then came Grandpapa more slowly, and after him stepped Grandmamma very sedately. Grandmamma never did anything in a hurry. This was not because she was old; it was because she was old-fashioned.

"Here we all are, safe and sound!" cried Grandpapa, kissing everybody who came within reach.

"I am sure I wonder we are here at all," said Grandmamma. "I have never travelled in so strange a coach."

"We thought you would like to be fetched in the new motor-car," said the Squire, giving her his arm.

"I thought it was a railway train," said Grandmamma.

THE CHRISTMAS GUESTS ARRIVE

HANGING UP THE STOCKINGS ✒ ✒

GOING to bed becomes a pleasure on Christmas Eve, because, as everybody knows, bed makes the next day come quicker. Besides, there are the stockings to hang up.

"I wonder if the biggest stockings get the most presents," said Pat.

"I hope not," said Elfie, looking at her own, which were the shortest.

"The best children get the most presents," said Nurse.

"Are we best children?" wondered Pat, anxiously.

"That depends on whether we are written in Santa Claus's Book of Good Children," said Nancy.

"Oh dear," sighed Pat. "I hit Baby on the head for bursting my new air-ball, yesterday."

Elfie ran to the chimney and called up it as loudly as she could: "Please, Santa Claus, leave your Book of Bad Children at home, and don't forget my dolly with the blue eyes."

Cousin Bob, who was big enough to do his own hair and compound long division, burst out laughing. "You funny children!" he cried. "Do you mean to say that you believe in Santa Claus?"

There was complete silence in the night nursery when

Cousin Bob said this. The children were too surprised to speak at first. Then Elfie looked over her shoulder, and said in a shocked tone: " Oh, hush, Bob! Something dreadful will happen to you if you talk like that."

" I don't care," said Bob. But he felt a little uneasy, all the same.

THE GREAT SECRET ♪ ♪ ♪

P AT," said Nancy in a loud whisper, "go and see if all is safe."

Pat crept on tiptoe to the top of the stairs and came back to say that no one was in sight. Nancy went to the night nursery cupboard and brought out a brown paper parcel, and they all stood round it in their night-gowns. Then the paper was taken off, and they had a last look at the present they had bought for Father and Mother. It was a picture of the children, Baby and all, framed in red leather; and it was

a tremendous surprise, for no one but Nurse even knew that it had been taken.

"I hope Mother won't notice that Baby screwed up his mouth," said Pat.

"I hope Father will see how well Sophia has come out," said Nancy.

"Doesn't my new frock look pretty?" said Elfie.

Then the picture was put back again into the brown paper, and not a moment too soon; for just then, there came a step on the landing, and Mother came right into the room. However, she did not seem to notice anything unusual, though Pat rushed to the cupboard in a great hurry, and the two girls looked very red in the face.

"You did not hear anything funny, did you, Mother?" enquired Elfie.

"I can hear Baby splashing in his bath," said Mother; and this was a great relief to everyone. Baby, in his bath, made far more noise than any brown paper parcel.

BABY'S STOCKING

WHEN they went in to say good-night to Baby, they found him hanging up his stocking. It was really only a sock, but that was more than he could manage by himself.

"Keeps tumbling down," he grumbled. "Naughty sock!"

It was a little difficult for the sock to do anything else, as Baby only put it on the edge of his cot and expected it to hang there by itself. Even on Christmas Eve a stocking will not hang up by itself.

Nancy pinned it on with a safety pin, and then it did not tumble down any more. "There!" she said. "If you are a good boy, Santa Claus will bring you ever so many Christmas presents."

"I am a good boy," said Baby, beaming all over. "Where are the presents?"

"They will come when Baby is asleep," explained Mother. "Santa Claus will drive in his sledge* from the ice mountains, and then he will climb on to the roof and come down the chimney and fill Baby's stocking with presents."

"Will he be all dirty?" said Baby.

*Another word for "sleigh."

"Oh no," said Mother. " He will be white like snow and glistening like frost. Nothing, not even a smoky chimney, will make him black."

"Shall we be in his Book of Good Children, do you think?" asked Pat.

"I shall be very disappointed if you are not," said Mother.

This made them all feel a little anxious. It would be dreadful if they had to disappoint Mother as well as go without their presents.

"I'm a very good boy," again proclaimed the Baby in a loud voice. He was not at all anxious.

"What can we do to make sure of being good enough?" wondered Elfie.

"You can see who will be in bed first," said Nurse, who always took advantage of remarks of this kind.

Pat jumped into the nearest bed, which was Cousin Bob's.

"That does not count," said Nurse, severely.

"I am glad Nurse is not Santa Claus," thought Pat.

THE WAITS

IT is not easy to sleep with one eye open, though, no doubt, it can be done with practice. Unfortunately, Nancy had not had enough practice to do it properly; so when she tried to keep awake for Santa Claus with one eye and to go to sleep with the other, she ended in keeping awake alto-gether. This was all the more provoking, as Sophia, who never closed either of her eyes, day or night, was sleeping soundly beside her.

Suddenly, the sound of music came up from the garden below. It sounded very far-away and sweet and soft, and it was difficult to make out any particular tune, and it was all rather mysterious. At least, so Nancy thought, as she opened both eyes and sat up in bed to listen. Elfie heard it, too, though she had been sound asleep the minute before; and she sat up and blinked her eyes and wondered if it were Christmas morning. Then she saw the moonlight squeezing itself in at the window, and she knew it was still Christmas Eve.

"Nancy!" she whispered.   "Is it the bells on Santa Claus's reindeer?"

"No," said Nancy.   "I think it must be the Christmas angels, 'cos I can hear harps."

Then Cousin Bob and Pat crept in on tiptoe.   "I say, you two, have you heard the waits?" asked Bob, in great excitement.

"Yes, listen to the waits,"* added Cousin Sylvia, coming in at another door.   "There's a bass viol, and two fiddles, and a harp."

Of course, Sylvia was nearly as old as Bob, and that was

*Street musicians who play at night during the Christmas season.

[32]

why she knew the difference between waits and reindeer bells. But when Nurse had come in and packed them all off to bed again, and the waits had gone away, and everything was still once more, Elfie wondered if they had known so much about it after all. "I don't think they were waits," she murmured sleepily; "I believe it was Santa Claus all the time, and I will stay awake to see." Unfortunately, she dropped asleep as she was saying this.

Then Nancy, who had been wider awake than ever since the waits came, felt she could not stay in bed another minute. So first she put one foot out of bed, then she put the other foot out, and then she pattered across the floor to the window. She pulled the blind a tiny bit on one side and peeped out.

She thought she had never seen anything so beautiful before. The garden did not look a bit like the everyday garden that she knew; it was all white and shining with snow and moonlight and frost; and the trees had queer shapes, as if they had left their daylight shapes behind them when the sun went down; and the gravel paths looked friendly

[33]

and inviting, as if they led straight to Fairyland; and the lawn looked like a big sheet of paper waiting for the Fairy Queen to come and write something on it; and over it hung the most wonderful silence, not at all like the silence that Nurse sometimes insisted upon when there was too much noise, but a silence that was like music.

"It is all waiting for Santa Claus," thought Nancy. "If I wait too, perhaps I shall see him come."

But Santa Claus did not come; and Nancy remembered that he never came until all little boys and girls were in bed, so she let the blind drop back into its place and crept into bed again. In half a minute more she was sound asleep with both eyes shut.

Just at that moment, Santa Claus was shutting up his Book of Good and Bad Children with a chuckle. It had taken him nearly all day to read, for there are a great many children in the world, when they are all added together, and there is a good deal to be said about each. But Santa Claus did not seem tired.

"I have not spent such a pleasant Christmas Eve for a thousand years," he said.

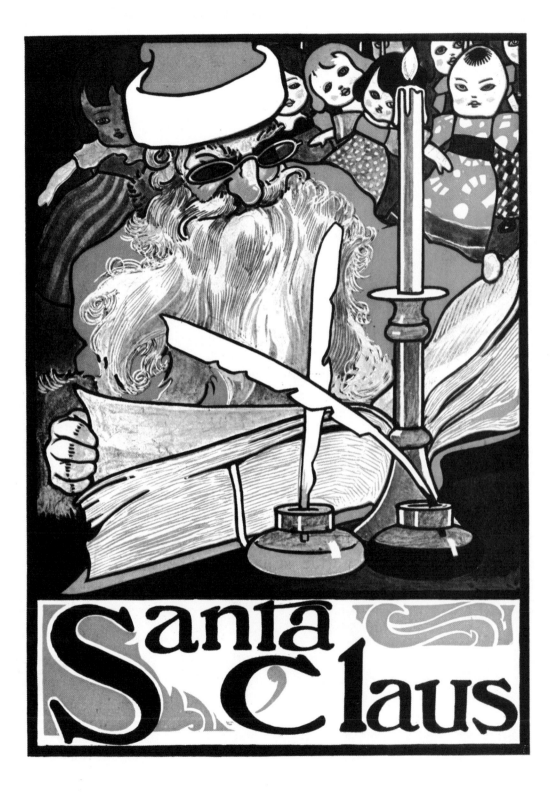

SANTA CLAUS AT HOME

FAR away among the peaks of the snow mountains, where no children play and the sunbeams have to shine without being told how pretty they are, Santa Claus keeps his toy-shop. It is not like an ordinary toy-shop. Just between the two biggest peaks of all there is a wide still valley, hung all over with icicles; and from every icicle hangs a toy. Nobody has ever been there; it is just a secret between Santa Claus and the sunbeams. And once a year, Santa Claus goes into his toy-shop with a big smile on his face.

"Ha, ha!" said Santa Claus, rubbing his hands, as he looked over his enormous glittering toy-shop. "Nearly

midnight, and I have not begun
to load up yet!" Then he opened
his Book of Good Children, just
to refresh his memory, and began
to fill his bag with toys. But
when he came to Pat, he consulted his book again, and his
great big smile grew a tiny bit
smaller.

"He did hit the Baby on the
head," he said sorrowfully, as he
picked up a knife with two blades
and a corkscrew. Then he consulted the Book of Good
Children once more, and his smile stretched a little.

"Hurrah!" he cried. "He kissed the Baby afterwards
and gave him a new air-ball of his own. Pat shall have the
knife without the corkscrew!"

LOADING UP

WHEN Santa Claus had filled his bag up to the top, he stopped smiling just long enough to give a low clear whistle, that sped right across the valley and curled round and round the mountain tops till it was lost among the snows. Then he stood still and waited. And after a moment there came a faint sound of bells, right away in the distance, and it came nearer and nearer and nearer, until round the corner dashed two magnificent reindeer, pulling a silver sledge behind them. They were so glad to see their master that they shook their fairy bells at him, and nestled their noses in his hand, and looked at him with their big brown eyes as if they were saying "A happy Christmas" with all their might.

"A happy Christmas to you, too, my beauties," said Santa Claus, who, of course, knew what their big brown eyes were saying. Then he emptied his bag of toys inside the sledge and

went back for more. He was
very careful over all the toys,
but he seemed particularly
careful about a large dolly with
blue eyes and curly hair.
"Elfie loves the
fairies," he said, as
he laid her present
gently on the seat.

The silver sledge
that belongs to
Santa Claus was
made in Fairy-
land. That is why
it holds enough
toys for all the
children in the
world, and always
has room for just
one more as well. This was very lucky, as it happened; for
just as Santa Claus was getting into the sledge, he remembered that he had put in nothing for Cousin Sylvia.

"Dear me," he said, "I must be getting old!" Then he
went back and found three beautiful story-books for Sylvia,
and packed them into the sledge. "I almost wish I were
a child myself," said Santa Claus, as he stepped in among
the toys.

And his smile grew bigger than ever.

ON THE WAY

IF Santa Claus's sledge were not a fairy sledge, it would make such a clatter as it raced along over hilltops and through valleys and across rivers and seas, that nobody would be able to sleep on the night before Christmas Day! And if his reindeer were not fairy reindeer, they would never be able to get all round the world and back to the snow mountains again before dawn, without so much as getting out of breath. But Fairyland arranges these things beautifully; and the smile on the face of Santa Claus just grew bigger and bigger and bigger as he sat among his toys and let the reindeer with the big brown eyes take him from one end of the world to the other, stopping on the way at every house that had any children inside. It was not long before dawn when he at last came to a standstill in the garden of the old Hall.

It was all as still as it had been when Nancy looked out of the window, except that the air was filled now with the sound of fairy bells. But they did not wake anybody up. Fairy bells only bring nice dreams to people, without waking them up.

Santa Claus filled his wonderful bag for the last time,

swung it over his shoulder, and climbed up to the roof. For a man who is over a thousand years old, Santa Claus is wonderfully active. Of course, if he liked, he could easily come in through the key-hole instead of down the chimney, which would be much less exhausting; but he would never dream of doing anything so silly.

"Christmas comes but once a year," said Santa Claus with a chuckle, as he tucked his cloak round him and squeezed himself, toys and all, into the night-nursery chimney-pot. He found it such a tight fit that he was rather glad Christmas did not come oftener than once a year.

IN THE NIGHT NURSERY ❧

IT is not easy to put a beautiful waxen lady, dressed in pink silk and covered from top to toe with pink frills, into a stocking as small as Elfie's without crumpling her frock; but Santa Claus managed it somehow. And anybody else would have found it difficult to balance a doll's perambulator, painted white and filled with pale-blue cushions, on the end of Nancy's bed, without waking either Nancy or Sophia. But Santa Claus managed this too. He also succeeded in squeezing more picture-books and sweets and crackers and balls and tops and whips and trumpets and whistles into all the stockings than anybody else could believe possible. We must remember, however, that he has been

doing this sort of thing every Christmas for the last thousand years; so he has had plenty of practice.

When Santa Claus came to Pat's stocking, his smile, if possible, grew a little bigger than before; in fact, it travelled so far round his head that it got lost in his white hair. For Pat looked so good and jolly and happy and pleasant in his sleep, that it was difficult to believe he had ever hit anybody on the head.

"I half wish I had not left out the corkscrew," sighed Santa Claus, as he popped the knife with the two blades into Pat's stocking. Then, to make up for the corkscrew, he put an extra number of smaller presents on the top of the knife, not forgetting a particularly fine regiment of soldiers with a camp fire and six tents and a big gun.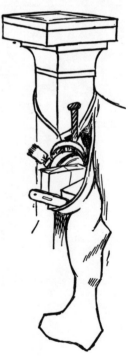

"I don't think he will mind much about the corkscrew," said Santa Claus, as he shouldered his bag of toys and went into the cousins' bed-room.

Pat smiled in his sleep. He did not look as if he would mind.

HANGING UP THE STOCKINGS

Page 26

THE WAITS

Page 31

THE BABY'S LETTER

WHEN the cousins' stockings were all filled, there only remained the Baby's. This, although the smallest of all, was by no means the least important. There it hung from the end of Baby's cot, just as Nancy had pinned it; and it looked as though it were asking for Christmas presents at the top of its voice. That was just what Baby had been doing, up the chimney, for the last week; so Santa Claus knew quite well what he was expected to put into Baby's stocking. But in case there should be any mistake about it, Baby had pinned a letter on to the top of his stocking, and addressed it to Santa Claus, just to remind him. Santa Claus chuckled when he opened it; for although the letter was supposed to be from Baby, it was easy to guess, from the spelling, that Pat had written it. This is what was in the letter:—

Dear Santa Claus nurse says i am a good boy so i can have a Chrismas pressent pleese I want a big drum and a bakers cart and a punk ball. i hope you are quite well now. i must say good-bi your lovving litel friend Baby

Santa Claus folded up the letter and put it in his pocket—his pockets are full of letters like that, and some of them are a thousand years old—and then he dived into his bag and pulled out a big drum, and a baker's cart, and a pink ball; and, strange though it may sound, he put them all into Baby's stocking. This, of course, could only be done at Christmas-time; at any other time, no stocking, not even a grown-up one, would have held so much as one of Baby's presents.

"That's done," said Santa Claus, as he flung his empty bag over his shoulder and went up the chimney again.

The chimney was not such a tight fit this time, because there was only Santa Claus in it, and his bag was empty. But he was not sorry when he stood once more on the white roof of the old Hall, looking down at the white silent garden.

SANTA CLAUS AND HIS REINDEER

BACK TO THE MOUNTAINS

TO travel from one end of the world to the other between midnight and dawn, and to climb up and down hundreds and hundreds of chimneys on the way, is a most exhausting way of spending the night.

"Ah, well," said Santa Claus with a yawn, as he flew home in his fairy sledge, "Christmas comes but once a year, and I've got a whole twelvemonth to sleep it off!"

The fairy reindeer flew over hills and through valleys and across rivers and seas; and just as the first gleams of dawn were turning the snow mountains pink at the edges, they brought Santa Claus to his home.

"A merry Christmas to you!" said Santa Claus, as the reindeer trotted off to rest for another year. Then he sat down in the middle of his toy-shop and listened.

He listened and listened and listened. And presently, when the sun was shining brightly over the whole world, as it only can shine on Christmas Day, he heard thousands and thousands of children laughing and chattering, and chattering and laughing, as they opened their Christmas presents.

"That's good enough for me," chuckled Santa Claus, as he pulled on his nightcap and went to sleep.

WAKING ON CHRISTMAS MORNING

Christmas Day

"A MERRY CHRISTMAS, a merry Christmas, a merry Christmas!" rang the Christmas bells across the snow.

Elfie kept her eyes shut tight, because she thought they were the fairy bells on the reindeer of Santa Claus; but Nancy sat up in bed and rubbed the sleep out of her eyes, and Pat suddenly gave a great shout. "It's Christmas Day!" he cried; and, just as he said this, Baby marched in at the door of the night nursery, beating his new drum, and after that there was no more sleep for anybody.

"Merry Christmasses, merry Christmasses!" shouted Baby, and he hammered mightily on his drum till Nurse came and took it away from him.

"Come and play with your baker's cart instead," she said coaxingly. "That's a nice quiet toy."

"I like loud toys best," said Baby, and, finding that his drum was gone, he thumped the floor with his drum-stick instead. Fortunately, he was just of that height at which it did not make much difference to him whether he hit the floor or his new drum.

Christmas Day is the most beautiful day in the whole year on which to awake. It is ever so much better than a birthday, because only one person has presents on a birthday. It is like a birthday for the whole world, and that is why it makes everybody feel good and happy and jolly. It would be very difficult to feel cross on Christmas Day; and I never heard of anybody who quarrelled on it.

"Why are the bells ringing like that?" said Elfie.

"Like what?" asked Nancy, who was still rubbing her eyes.

"As if they were laughing," said Elfie.

"I suppose they know it is Christmas Day," said Nancy.

"Bells do not laugh," said Nurse. "Bells ring."

"I think they laugh when they are Christmas bells," said Elfie.

WHAT SANTA CLAUS BROUGHT

I'VE been expecting you," whispered Elfie, as she hugged her new dolly; and she examined it carefully to make sure that the pink silk frock would unfasten, and that the flaxen hair was real and could be properly combed and plaited, and that other important matters of this kind had not been neglected by Santa Claus.

"Please be careful what you say before Sophia," advised Nancy from the next bed. "Sophia is inclined to be jealous. Still, if you introduce her properly, we will invite her to come for a drive in Sophia's new perambulator."

"Dolls! What's the good of dolls?" cried Cousin Bob, rushing in with his new gun. "Just look at this!"

"And this! And this!" cried everybody at once.

THE BOYS' PRESENTS

AFTER that there was such a clatter of voices and laughter, and such a crackling of paper parcels, that Nurse mentioned baths three times without being heard. But it was Christmas morning, so, of course, she was not cross.

"Do you believe in Santa Claus now, Bob?" asked Elfie anxiously.

Bob stroked his new gun affectionately, and felt a tiny bit ashamed of the things he had said over-night about Santa Claus. "Anyhow, he knows jolly well what a fellow wants," he admitted, which was quite enough for Elfie.

Pat sat up in bed, surrounded with presents, and silent with joy. "It has two blades," he murmured at last under his breath.

"Didn't you ask for a corkscrew too, Pat?" cried Nancy.

"Oh, no!" said Pat, who had quite forgotten about the corkscrew. That is how Santa Claus arranges these things.

SINGING A CAROL AT MOTHER'S DOOR

WAKING FATHER
AND MOTHER

"I WONDER if Father and Mother are awake yet," said Nancy.

Then Cousin Sylvia, who was old enough to think of new and interesting things to do, caught sight of the robins singing on the window ledge; and she said:—"Let us go and sing carols outside their door."

So they all crept on tiptoe along the passage, to make it more of a surprise, and then they stood in a row outside the bed-room door and sang "Good King Wenceslas", as the village girls and boys had sung it in the garden, the day before. The carol grew much louder in the second verse, because Pat, who was always a little late for everything, did not join them till they had finished singing the first verse, and then he came in a great

hurry with only one shoe on.   But that, fortunately, did not spoil his voice in any way.

"I wonder if they are awake yet," said Nancy, when they had finished.

"Let us sing another carol, to make sure," said Sylvia.

So they sang another carol to make sure, and after that another one, and after that one more.

"They must be awake now," said Pat, who was growing hungry and wished that they could have plum-cake and fizzy ginger-beer for a reward, like the village carol singers.

Then Baby, who could not sing carols, made up for this by beating a loud tattoo on his new drum, which made them all put their fingers in their ears.

"They will never go to sleep again, I should think!" said Bob, who much preferred air-guns to drums.

PRESENTS FOR THE KITCHEN

"ARE you ready?" asked Nancy. Elfie and Pat and Baby nodded—their hands were so full of parcels that they could not speak, for fear of dropping something,— then they made a little procession, one behind another, and marched downstairs to the kitchen. There was a present from each of them to everybody in the kitchen, from Cook down to Tommy the garden-boy; and it was difficult to wait for the parcels to be opened, so anxious were the children to point out what nice presents were inside.

"I wanted to give you a bright red handkerchief with yellow spots, Tommy," said Pat; "but Mother said plain white ones were more useful."

"I chose you a china cat with a pink face, Cook," chimed in Elfie; "but Mother strongly advised this workbox instead."

"Baby wanted to give you his wooden horse without a tail, Sarah, because he is so fond of you," said Nancy; "but we persuaded him to give you some gloves instead. I hope you like Baby's present; do you?"

"I don't like it," said Baby, throwing it at Sarah. "Take it away." Sarah was quite ready to take it away. She liked gloves better than wooden horses, for a Christmas present.

The children stood in a row and looked on while Cook, and Sarah, and Tommy, opened their parcels and said "Thank you". Cook and Sarah were very pleased with their presents, but Tommy was a little doubtful about his. He would have liked a bright red handkerchief with yellow spots.

Then there came a yell from Cousin Bob, who was keeping watch on the door-step, and they all rushed out just in time to meet the Christmas postman.

THE POSTMAN

THE CHRISTMAS POST 🙟 🙟

O N any other morning in the year, the poor postman would feel very sorry for himself if he had to carry so many letters; but on Christmas Day, everybody is so glad to see him that he feels quite important, and that is always a pleasant feeling on any morning in the year.

The Hall was the last house on the postman's round; so, when he had emptied his bag there, Sarah told him he was to come into the kitchen and have a good breakfast and a warm before he went home again.

"I've had my breakfast," said Baby, who could not think why the postman had not had his. "I don't want any breakfast. Look at my drum."

"That's a fine drum, that is," said the postman. But he went in to breakfast, all the same. One cannot breakfast off a fine drum, even on Christmas Day.

Father and Mother and Grandpapa and Grandmamma were still having breakfast when the children took in the Christmas letters. There was kissing all round the table when

they appeared; and they all
said "A Merry Christmas"
at once, so that, if people
had not known what was
being said, they could not
possibly have guessed what
it was. It is only on Christmas Day that people can all
talk at once without being
impolite.

Then the Squire sorted
the big pile of letters in
front of him, and Elfie trotted round the table and gave
them to the right people.
There were Christmas cards
for everyone, even for Baby,
who had one big one all to
himself, with a robin on it.
Mother had twenty-two, and some of them were very grand.
But the ones she liked best of all were four small ones
that had been addressed to her in the nursery, on Christmas Eve.

"Clever postman, to bring Mummy Baby's Christmas
card!" cried Baby, when he saw that his card had really
arrived.

When Father saw the way Baby's card was addressed,
he agreed with Baby.

GOING TO CHURCH

AFTER breakfast there was a great scramble to get ready for church. There were so many boots to be buttoned, so many coats to be fastened, and so many gloves to put on, that it did not seem at first as if anybody could be ready in time. It is wonderful, though, what can be done with a little help and a great deal of good temper; and, fortunately, Sylvia was almost as quick as Nurse in dressing people. Of course she was older than Nancy or Elfie, and could read the longest words without spelling them first, and had grown up into kid gloves with two buttons, so she ought to have been what Nurse called her—a handy little girl.

From all the houses in the town little processions of

fathers and mothers and children came pouring out to go to church; but the biggest procession of all was the one that came from the Hall. That was because of Grandpapa and Grandmamma and the cousins, of course.

"This reminds me of old times," said Grandpapa, as he saw the people trudging through the snow.

"Times have changed since I was a girl," said Grandmamma with a sigh. Nobody felt sad, though, when Grandmamma said this. For one thing, she said it so often that people had grown used to hearing it; and for another, nobody quite believed that Grandmamma ever had been a girl.

On the way to church there were several Christmas presents to be left at the cottage doors—a new coat for neighbour Bunce, a woollen shawl for old Mrs. Munger, and a packet of sweets and toys for the little Mungers, besides ever so many more that Mother had been making into parcels for days and days. This was all very pleasant, because it kept up the nice Christmasy feeling all the way to church, and quite prevented anybody from mistaking it for an ordinary Sunday.

"Just the same as when I was a boy!" cried Grandpapa, as he saw the parcels being left, one by one, at the cottage doors.

"It does not recall to me the same period," said Grand-

mamma, as a motor-car whizzed past.

"When you were a girl, Grandmamma, did people dress in armour?" asked Pat.

"Was gunpowder invented, when you were a girl, Grandmamma?" asked Bob.

"Did you ever meet Queen Elizabeth, Grandmamma, when you were a girl?" asked Nancy.

Grandpapa roared with laughter when he heard these questions; but Grandmamma did not seem so much amused.

"Dear me!" she exclaimed. "Anybody might think I was an old woman!"

IN CHURCH

COUSIN SYLVIA was very useful during church time. She knew exactly where the right psalms were, and how to find the hymns; and Pat and Elfie, who had the greatest difficulty over matters of this kind, were very glad to sit on either side of her. As Elfie could not read, it did not really matter where she opened her hymn-book; but it made her feel much more grown-up to know that she was looking at the right page. For that matter, the place in the hymn-book is of no consequence to anybody on Christmas Day; for, of course, everybody can sing "Hark, the herald angels sing!" without a book at all.

The little old country church looked very beautiful with its Christmas decorations. There were garlands of evergreens twined round the big stone pillars, and wreaths of holly hanging on all the pews, and bunches of red berries all along the top of the dark oak pulpit. And the sun shone in through the painted glass of the windows, and cast pretty red and blue and purple lights across everything, till Elfie began to think that the church must have been altered a little, on purpose, for Christmas Day. "I think the Christmas angel came down in the night and painted all those pretty colours, don't you?" she whispered to Bob, as they came out of church.

"You are a funny little girl, aren't you?" said Cousin Bob. But he did not laugh at her, and that was saying a good deal —for Cousin Bob.

Then they all forgot everything else in the fun of meeting their friends outside church, and wishing them all sorts of good wishes, and telling and hearing all about the Christmas presents. For on Christmas Day you are just as excited over other people's presents as you are over your own; and you would never dream of wanting them as well as your own. No doubt, this is because Christmas presents come from Fairyland.

WALKING HOME FROM CHURCH

WALKING HOME ✤ ✤ ✤

THEY were not long walking home from church, because Father made them run races in the snow. It is great fun to run races in the snow, for as fast as you run forward you slip backward, and then the snow makes a lump of ice on your heel and you cannot stand upright at all. But it is the same for everybody, as Mother remarked when Father and Elfie fell down together. "I don't like being the same as everybody," said Elfie, rubbing her elbow.

One of the nicest things about walking home from church on Christmas Day is the jolly feeling of looking forward to everything that is going to happen. And the first thing that is going to happen is the Christmas dinner.

"Is it greedy to look forward to Christmas pudding?" wondered Pat, a little anxiously.

"It may be greedy," said Cousin Bob, "but I do look forward to it."

"It is not greedy to look forward to it," said Mother. "It is only greedy to eat too much of it, or to——"

No doubt Mother meant to say more about greediness, but just then Baby came running along the path to meet them, and he settled the question without any more ado.

"Plum-pudding! Plum-pudding for Baby and all!" shouted Baby, banging merrily on his new drum. Baby did not think it was greedy to look forward to plum-pudding.

GETTING READY FOR DINNER

CHARLES ROBINSON

GETTING ready for dinner is generally rather a bother. The soap gets into people's eyes. The comb pulls people's hair. It is very tiresome to have to stand still while somebody ties on a bib that tells the world, not always truthfully: "I am a good boy". It would be much pleasanter to go down to dinner without getting ready for it first. On Christmas Day, all this is altered. Getting ready for dinner becomes a pleasure. The soap never gets into people's eyes. The comb never pulls people's hair. Bibs are tied round people's necks as if by magic; and everybody is a good boy, unless anybody happens to be a good girl instead. There are only good fairies in the nursery on Christmas Day.

FATHER CARVING THE TURKEY

The Christmas Dinner

THE Christmas dinner lasted a long while. This was not because people ate so much, but because it took the Squire so long to carve the turkey for everyone. But there was so much conversation going on, that no one noticed how long it took.

The great event of the dinner was the Christmas pudding. All the blinds were pulled down before it came in, which Baby did not like. "Pull them up again," he said. "Don't want to go to bed."

Then the pudding was brought in, all blazing with blue flames; and it was easy to see why the blinds had been pulled down. But Baby did not see why, and he was not happy till they were pulled up again. "It isn't bed-time any more," he said, beaming with smiles.

The best fun of all was trying to eat the blue flames

as well as the pudding. It is not easy to eat blue flames
in a spoon. But it is quite easy to think that one can;
and that is much more important.

"I like eating flames," said Pat. "Flames taste of plums
and currants and peel."

"My flames taste of that, too," said Cousin Bob; which
made Pat feel very proud.

"You are not eating flames; you are just eating plum-
pudding," said Sylvia.

Nobody seemed to hear this remark of Cousin Sylvia's.

SINGING A CAROL AT MOTHER'S DOOR

Page 58

BRINGING IN THE PLUM PUDDING

Page 75

GRANDPAPA'S SPEECH ❧ ❧ ❧

EVERYBODY clapped and cheered when Grandpapa got up to make a speech. Grandpapa always made a speech on Christmas Day, and it was always the same speech. Nobody minded that, though. It is always pleasant to know what is coming, so long as it is something worth hearing.

"It makes me feel young again to see so many young faces around me," began Grandpapa. "When I was a boy, I used to come down to dinner on Christmas Day, and tuck into turkey and plum-pudding, just as you are doing. I dare say I was as fond of good things as any young rascal here——"

"My dear, I am sure you were not of a greedy disposition," said Grandmamma, as she always said every year.

"I was no better than the rest of 'em," chuckled Grandpapa, which immensely pleased all the boys in the room. "But times have changed, bless me! how times have changed since then! There were no new-fangled steam-engines running about your country roads then, with people inside 'em dressed up in furs like heathen Eskimos! The coach was good enough for us. Ah, those were merry times indeed! Two days and a night to get here from town, and a whole week if we got snowed up on the way. You fellows don't know what you've missed by being born too late. If you'd once sat on the box seat behind four spirited greys, with your fingers and toes dropping off with cold, and a chance of being held up by highwaymen every minute, you'd soon stop boasting about your motor-cars and your express trains. Give me a four-horse coach and the good old times back again!"

"That can never be, alas!" sighed Grandmamma. But she looked so contented as she said this, that Elfie could not help thinking that she did not really mind the new times, though people's fingers and toes did not drop off any more.

"Did they grow new ones when the old ones dropped off?" she wondered. Grandpapa's and Grandmamma's hands certainly had the right number of fingers on them.

THE MINCE PIES

GRANDPAPA'S speech had given everybody an appetite for the mince pies. This was a good thing, as it would be extremely difficult to eat a mince pie without an appetite. Indeed, when Grandmamma remarked that in her day, which seemed to have been about the period of the Wars of the Roses, the mince pies were twice as big as they are now, everybody felt rather glad that Grandmamma's day was over.

Baby had as large an appetite as anybody for the mince pies. This was unfortunate, as he was the only person at the table who was not allowed to have one. "Baby has had such a large dinner," said Mother. "I am sure he does not want a mince pie."

Baby was not of the same opinion as Mother. Though his dinner had been large, he would have liked it to be larger.

THE DOG'S CHRISTMAS DINNER

CHARLIE ROBINSON

IT is not greedy to enjoy eating one's Christmas dinner; but it would be very greedy to forget all about other people's Christmas dinners. Pat was not a greedy boy, so he remembered the dog's dinner.

"Do you think Jock would like a mince pie, as it is Christmas Day?" he wondered.

"I think he would prefer some scraps of turkey and a nice lot of biscuits and gravy," said Father.

So Pat mixed an extra good dinner for Jock, and took it out to him on the doorstep. Jock wagged his tail all the time he was eating it, which showed that he knew it was a Christmas dinner.

THE CAT'S CHRISTMAS DINNER

NANCY was not a greedy little girl, so she thought of the cat's dinner before she had finished her own. "May Pussy have some plum-pudding for a treat?" she whispered to Mother.

"She would much prefer some stale fish," said Mother. "Go and ask Cook if she has some scraps of fish for Pussy. Cats do not like the same kind of food as little girls."

"I am glad I am not a cat," said Elfie.

Pussy was glad she was not a little girl when she compared the nice, tasty, fishy dinner that Nancy and Elfie set before her, with the one that they had just been eating.

THE ROBINS'
CHRISTMAS DINNER

BABY also thought of other people before he finished his own dinner; but that may have been partly because he grew a little tired of his own dinner.

"Baby give his dinner to the dear little robins," he said, waving his spoon towards the window. "Baby can't eat any more."

This was not the best of reasons for being generous; but Mother overlooked this, as it was Christmas Day.

"Let us crumble up some bread for the robins, and we will put out some bits of meat for the blackbirds, and some pieces of sugar for a Christmas pudding," said Mother.

So the birds had their Christmas dinner as well as everybody else. They made a great deal of noise over it, but that may have been because it was Christmas Day. It is impossible not to talk at dinner-time on Christmas Day. Besides, no doubt some of them were making speeches.

WHEN GRANDPAPA WAS YOUNG

GRANDPAPA'S YOUNG DAYS

"IN my young days," said Grandpapa with a chuckle, "the mistletoe was what I liked best on Christmas Day."

Baby opened his eyes very wide at this. "Baby not allowed to eat mistletoes," he said sadly; and he thought Grandpapa must have been a very happy little boy in his young days, if his Nurse allowed him to eat mistletoe berries.

"Why did you like the mistletoe best, Grandpapa?" asked Elfie.

Grandpapa chuckled again. "Ask Grandmamma," he said.

Grandmamma shook her curls at him. "There is one Christmas Day I shall never forget," she said, which was certainly no answer to Elfie's question.

"Did you have such nice presents that day, Grandmamma?" asked Pat.

"I had the best present I ever had in my life, Pat," answered Grandmamma, which was the most puzzling thing that had been said yet, though it made Father and Mother laugh a good deal.

Then Grandpapa gave another huge chuckle, which shook the whole table. "The mistletoe hung just over the bottom

stair," he said; "and Grandmamma never noticed it as
she came downstairs to
where I stood waiting for
her. Do you remember, my
dear?"

Grandmamma shook her
curls again, and Grandpapa
went on to describe the
dress she had worn. "It
was a flowered silk, my
dears," he said, "and it
stood out round Grand-
mamma like a rosebush, and
she looked like the fairest
rose of all, growing up from
the middle of it."

"That's a way to describe a dress, indeed!" said Grandmamma. But she looked as though she rather liked it, all
the same.

"And then," Grandpapa went on, "she wore a hat, my
dears, that was exactly like that coal-scuttle over there."

"Were there any coals inside it?" asked Baby.

"There were only curls inside Grandmamma's hat,"
answered Grandpapa; "the prettiest curls you ever saw,
my dears."

"I don't see any curls in the coal-scuttle," said Baby.
"I can only see coals."

THE DESSERT

THE dessert is the most amusing part of the Christmas dinner. The other courses are only meant to be eaten; but when dessert comes, people can begin to play. And it is always more fun to play than to eat, though it is pleasant to do both.

Father could do lovely things with the dessert. He could play the battle of Trafalgar in a finger bowl with nut shells. He could make an orange into an old man with a row of giant's teeth and a horrible grin. The boys liked that; but Grandmamma said it frightened her, so Father cut the next orange into a pretty basket with a handle, and filled it with little pieces of orange covered over with white sugar. That pleased Grandmamma, and she showed the little girls how to make a raisin into a tea-pot, with a stalk for a handle and an almond for a spout. Then everybody made tea-pots, until Bob discovered how good the spouts were to eat; and after that, none of the tea-pots had any spouts left.

Then Pat took out his new knife and said he was going to turn a candied apricot into an old man. He worked very hard for some minutes, and grew very red and very sticky; but it did not look much like an old man when it was finished.

"If you had not told me what it was meant for, I should never have guessed," said Bob.

"I think it looks like a very nasty apricot," said Nancy.

CHARLESROBINSON

"It is not a nasty apricot," said Pat; and he ate it to show how good it was. He noticed that no one offered to share it with him.

"Some people are so particular," said Pat.

"Some people are not particular enough," said Nancy.

GRANDPAPA'S SONG

GRANDPAPA'S voice was not exactly a loud one. He did not sing deeply and gruffly, as Peter the gardener did; or in a shrill and lusty treble, as Tommy the garden-boy did in the choir on Sundays; or rather high and scrapily, as Nurse did, when she sang Baby to sleep. Grandpapa's voice was small and jerky, and he rocked himself about as he sang, and looked very fierce and important. But he paid far more attention to the tune than either Nurse or Peter did, and he said the words quite distinctly; so everybody was glad when he got up to sing his yearly song. Christmas would not have been Christmas without Grandpapa's song.

The children wondered why he chose such a funny song, this year. "Here's to the maiden of bashful fifteen!" sang Grandpapa in his faint, rollicking, old gentleman's voice; and although it was a pretty song, with lots of tune in it and a nice easy chorus, there was something distinctly odd about the words. There was no little girl so old as fifteen in the room—not even Sylvia; and as for the grown-up people in the song, neither Mother nor Grandmamma could have been called a "widow of fifty", or a "housewife that's thrifty".

Yet Grandpapa sang about all these people just as if he saw them sitting in front of him.

"A great song, a great song!" said Father, when Grandpapa sat down again. "Eh, Bob, my boy?"

Bob did not think so. He much preferred "Rule Britannia" or "The Bay of Biscay". But he was too polite to say so.

"I think it makes rather a fuss about a lot of people who are not here," he said. And that was what everyone in the room, who was under fifteen, thought too. But the people who were over fifteen only laughed.

AFTER DESSERT

WHEN dessert was over, Mother asked Grandmamma if she would like to rest on the drawing-room sofa for a little while.

"Oh, Grandmamma!" said Elfie, looking disappointed. "It would be much nicer to stay and roast chestnuts."

"When you get to my age, my dear," said Grandmamma, "you will know how much nicer it is to tuck yourself up for ten minutes after dinner."

"Grandpapa has got to your age, Grandmamma," Pat pointed out; "but he does not tuck himself up."

"Not I, my boy!" said Grandpapa, grandly. "No sofas for me! Six hours' sleep for a man, seven for a woman, eight for a fool."

"We are all fools then," said Bob, after doing a sum in his head.

Mother at once said that one way out of this difficulty would be to get up earlier in the morning. Mother knew how many times Bob had to be called in the morning before he went to his bath. This made Bob rather sad, until Pat thought of a still better way out of the difficulty.

"Let us all stay up later in the evening, instead," he said. "We should all be men, then!"

Mother did not seem to think much of Pat's plan. "You would not grow up at all, if you did that," she said.

"Then what are we to do, Grandpapa?" asked Bob.

But there came no answer from Grandpapa. He had fallen sound asleep in his chair. No sofas for Grandpapa!

It was very difficult not to smile when Grandpapa was discovered asleep in his chair. Still, a great deal could be done by looking in the opposite direction and winking both eyes hard; so nobody did smile.

"Everybody makes mistakes sometimes," whispered Sylvia.

"Grandpapa is very old," Nancy whispered back; "he must be a hundred at least. That is why he wants more than eight hours' sleep."

"Of course!" said everybody in the loudest whisper of all.

FAIRY TALES

THERE would be something very wrong with Christmas Day, if people did not sit round the fire and tell fairy tales.

"The fire is full of fairies on Christmas Day," said Elfie, looking into the deep red caves under the Yule log.

"I don't see any fairies," said Cousin Bob. "Those are just holes in the fire."

"Oh, no!" said Mother. "Do you not see the Fire King in the middle, and the little Fire Queen, dancing about her palace, and all the little fire fairies round her? She is looking for her son, the Prince, who has gone to find a Princess in the Land of the Burning Forest, on the borders of Smokeland; and if he does not bring her back before tea-time, the Fire King is going to destroy the Fire Palace and everybody in it."

"Oh, where is the Prince? Show him to us!" cried the children.

"There he is," said Mother, "that blue flame flickering near the chimney; and that is his Princess, the little green flame by his side. They are trying hard to get home in time; but it is very difficult, because the King of Smokeland is sending out his smoke imps to stifle them on the way. They will never get home by tea-time!"

"Tea-time, my dears," said Nurse's voice at the door: and

she wondered why everybody groaned at such a pleasant announcement.

"Oh, dear!" sighed the children. "They will never get home in time."

Fortunately, Mother did something with the poker just in time, and the next minute, the little blue flame and the little green flame went flying up the chimney. "Hurrah!" cried Elfie. "The Prince and Princess have escaped!"

Then the Fire Palace fell in with a blaze, and everybody went up to the nursery to tea.

CHARLES ROBINSON.

ROASTING CHESTNUTS 🦢 🦢

IT is splendid fun to roast chestnuts when the Christmas
dinner is over. There is no need to be hungry in order
to enjoy roasting chestnuts; for when you have taken off
the shell and the part that is burnt, there is very little
left, and that little is generally enough to take away anybody's appetite.

Mother enjoyed roasting chestnuts as well as anybody.
She liked putting them on the bars of the grate, and seeing
them fall into the fire, and fishing them out again with the
tongs, and pretending to eat little hard bits of them with a
great deal of salt to take out the taste.

LIGHTING THE CANDLES

THE furniture in the big drawing-room had been cleared away. The carpet had been taken away, too; and the boards had been polished. Everything was ready for blindman's-buff, and a red fire glowed in the wide open grate, when Father came in to light the candles, after tea. A great many people came to help Father, which, of course, was most kind and thoughtful of them. It is true that most of them were too short to reach the candles, and Father would not allow any of them to touch the taper. Still, there are many ways of helping; so some of them held the matches, and the others had slides on the polished boards, all of which was most helpful.

"Have we helped you, Father?" asked Pat, when all the candles were lit.

"I do not know what I should have done without you," said Father.

"I like helping people!" cried Baby, who had been running round Father's legs all the time.

It is very pleasant to feel, on Christmas Day, that people cannot get on without us.

BLINDMAN'S-BUFF

THE SNAPDRAGON

IT was quite dark in the dining-room. Everybody crowded round the dining-room table. Baby held Mother's hand very tight. He was not frightened, of course; brave boys are never afraid of the dark. Still, it was very comforting to feel that Mother was there.

"I wonder if the dragons will have wings," said Elfie.

"There are no dragons," said Bob; "there are only lighted plums."

"Then why is it called snapdragon?" asked Nancy.

Cousin Bob did not know, so he changed the subject. "When is it going to begin?" he asked, as if he had not heard Nancy's question.

"Hark!" said Mother.

There was a dead silence. Then something scraped and spluttered and scratched, and the next minute a large dish of blue flame blazed in the middle of the table.

"Oh, how pretty!" cried all the girls, clapping their hands.

"See how brave I am!" cried all the boys, as they dipped their fingers in the flames and tried to pull out the plums. No doubt, they were brave, but they did not pull out many plums; and when they did, they dropped them again immediately. It is not easy to hold a burning plum in one's fingers.

Cousin Sylvia did not say she was brave, but she put in her fingers and pulled out the plums quite calmly, one by one, instead of in handfuls. Cousin Sylvia became very popular in the next few minutes; for she blew out the plums and gave them to people to eat, which was much better than flinging them about the table just anyhow, as the boys did.

"I think they look pretty, but they are very nasty to eat," said Nancy.

Then the flames died down, and it was all dark again. "The dragons have gone back to Fairyland," sighed Elfie.

GRANDPAPA'S GAME

FROM the middle of the drawing-room ceiling hung a large bough of mistletoe; and under the mistletoe stood Grandmamma. This was quite accidental; for she was not wearing her spectacles, and she did not see the mistletoe. She just happened to stand there, because it was such a good place from which to watch the Christmas games.

Then Grandpapa played his Christmas game. It was very mean of him to take Grandmamma by surprise.

"You naughty boy!" she exclaimed, which seemed a most astonishing remark to make to an old gentleman, who was nearly eighty.

HUNT THE SLIPPER 👞 👞 👞

IT was not at all easy to hide the slipper when it was Grandpapa's slipper that was brought to the cobbler to be mended. There was something about Grandpapa's slipper that seemed to make it grow bigger every minute. So, although the girls spread out their skirts, and the boys threw it from side to side as fast as they could, it was soon found and given back to Grandpapa, who was very glad to have it, as his foot felt cold without it. Then everybody wanted to be the cobbler, which caused a little delay in the game. For some minutes, nothing could be heard but loud disputing. This occasionally happens in any kind of game; but it ought not to happen on Christmas Day. Sylvia felt this very strongly.

" Dear me," she said; " is this a game or a quarrel?"

This made everybody laugh.

" I don't want to be the cobbler," said Pat.

" Nor I! Nor I!" cried the others.

" I do," said Baby.

So Baby lent his slipper to be hunted. The difficulty with Baby's slipper was that it was too small to be found Even the people who were hiding it did not always know where it was. At last, it disappeared altogether. The cobbler had lost it, everybody had lost it, and the game had to come to an end.

"Where can Baby's slipper be?" cried everybody.

"Here!" said Baby, who was walking about with both slippers on.

Baby's foot had grown cold without his slipper, too.

CHARADES ✣ ✣ ✣ ✣

THE best part of acting charades is the dressing up. Mother was a great help at this part. She could turn Elfie into a shopman, and Cousin Bob into a sailor, and Sylvia into a soldier, and Pat into an engine-driver, without any trouble at all.

Sylvia was a great help at the acting part. "We must think of a word," she said. "How would 'Baby' do? 'Bay' and 'buy', don't you see?"

Nobody did see, but that did not matter. Sylvia told everybody what to do, and the audience was pleased, which was the great thing. Cousin Bob made a splendid sailor, and sang "The Bay of Biscay" to bring in the first syllable of the word; and Elfie made a splendid shopman, and sold Christmas presents from a shop made of the drawing-room chairs, to bring in the word "buy"; and then, amid a round of applause in which Grandpapa and Father made the most noise, because they had the biggest hands, all the actors retired to the hall to invent something for the whole word.

"Let me be the mother," suggested Nancy.

"And let my new dolly be the baby," said Elfie.

"We don't want a lot of dolls," objected Bob.

"Can you think of anything better?" demanded Sylvia.

When it came to the point, Cousin Bob could not think of anything at all. Things were, in fact, becoming rather difficult, when Baby suddenly settled the question by marching into

the drawing-room and announcing to the audience at the top of his voice: "I'm the word, I am! Look at me! Mummy, why am I the word? What does Sylvie mean?"

And that was the end of the charade.

HONEY POTS

CHARLES ROBINSON

I LIKE being a honey pot," said Baby, when Nancy and Elfie weighed him and sold him to Mother for two-pence. "May I be a honey pot always?"

"I should like you to be my Baby sometimes," said Mother. Baby did not agree with Mother; he would sooner be a honey pot always.

Everybody was a honey pot in turn, till there was no one left to buy the honey but Father. Then he said he was going to be a honey pot, too; but no one was big enough to weigh him, so he was never bought, and that game came to an end, too. "I will be a jam pot now," said Baby. Unfortunately, just as he said this, he slipped on the polished boards, and sat down by mistake.

After that, he was very glad to be Mother's Baby again.

GRANDMAMMA'S SONG

IT is impossible to play games all the evening, even on Christmas Day; so, just when everybody was feeling very hot and out of breath, Mother had a grand idea. She asked Grandmamma to sing a song.

"Yes, my dear," said Grandpapa, beaming all over; "sing them 'The Mistletoe Bough'."

Grandmamma said it was too sad; but they all said they liked sad songs best, so she stood up by the piano and sang them the song of "The Mistletoe Bough", in a sweet, gentle, quavering voice that seemed to belong to lavender and rose leaves and old flower-gardens. As for Grandpapa, he stamped his foot and nodded his head to keep time with the music.

GRANDMAMMA'S STORY

IT is very difficult, unless you are grown-up, to hear all the words in a song; so, when Grandmamma had finished singing, the children asked her to tell them the story of "The Mistletoe Bough" without any music.

"Once upon a time," began Grandmamma, "there was a young and beautiful girl, who was engaged to be married to a young and handsome man."

"There isn't going to be any kissing in the story, is there?" asked Cousin Bob anxiously.

Grandmamma did not notice this interruption. "And the

KISSING BABY UNDER THE MISTLETOE

Page 113

PREPARING FOR THE SNOW-BALL FIGHT

Page 138

"THE YOUNG BRIDE WENT UPSTAIRS TO HIDE"

night before the wedding" she went on, "there were great rejoicings in the house—dancing and games and all sorts of fun. Amongst other things, they played at hide-and-seek. Then a strange and terrible thing happened."

"What happened, Grandmamma?" asked everybody breathlessly.

"The young bride went upstairs to hide," said Grandmamma solemnly; "and she was never found."

"Never, Grandmamma?" gasped everybody.

"A hundred years later," said Grandmamma, shaking her head sorrowfully, "they opened an old oak chest in the attic, and there they found her skeleton. She must have hidden there, shut the lid, and then been unable to lift it again. Poor young thing!"

"I think the others were very stupid not to think of looking in the chest," said Cousin Bob.

"Perhaps," said Nancy, "it was somebody else's skeleton all the while. Do you think it was, Grandmamma?"

Grandmamma did not seem to think much of these remarks of Bob and Nancy.

HIDE-AND-SEEK ❦ ❦ ❦

I THINK a good game of hide-and-seek will cheer us all up," said Mother, when Grandmamma's story was over.

Father and Grandpapa were the seekers, and they had such long arms that they ought to have caught everybody. This did not happen, however. For one thing, Grandpapa's legs were not so young as they had been; so when Pat jumped out of the landing cupboard, and slid down the balusters, Grandpapa could not follow him.

"Where can Baby be?" said Mother, suddenly.

"Let us look in the oak chest," said Nancy.

Sure enough, there was Baby, curled up inside the oak chest. "Go away!" roared Baby, who did not want to be found. "Wait till I'm a 'keleton!"

But Mother did not want to wait a hundred years for her Baby.

UNDER THE MISTLETOE

'VE been standing here such a long time," said Baby.

Nobody heard this remark at first, but when Baby repeated it at the top of his voice, everybody turned round. It is not usual, of course, to ask to be kissed under the mistletoe; but when the person who asks is very small, and has two big tears in his eyes, one forgets what is usual. So everybody in the room kissed Baby under the mistletoe, and the two big tears dried up and disappeared.

"I'm still standing under the mistletoe," said Baby, when he had been kissed by everybody.

"A polite little boy does not stand too long under the mistletoe," said Mother.

"I'm not a polite little boy," said Baby; "I like standing under mistletoes."

THE CHRISTMAS RECITATION

IT is not fair to leave all the entertaining to people who are over seventy years old; so, when everybody was again too hot to play, Elfie obligingly said she would recite "The boy stood on the burning deck". There was no difficulty about hearing the words when Elfie recited; for when she could not remember what came next, she said the same words over again until someone in the room reminded her of the right ones. That is the advantage of reciting a poem that everybody else knows.

"If you like," said Pat, when Elfie had finished, "I shall recite that poem to you over again."

Nobody, however, took advantage of Pat's offer.

THE PIANOFORTE PIECES &

A VERY important part of Christmas Day is hearing the children play their pieces. That is one of the things grown-up relations are there for. So, when Grandmamma said: "Nancy dear, will you play us a little tune?" it was only what Nancy had been expecting all the time.

It is rather frightening to sit down and play to a room full of people. It makes your hands wobble, and your breath feel jumpy; and you wish somebody else would play at the same time, so that the wrong notes might not all belong to you. However, Nancy did not feel frightened when she saw how friendly everybody was looking; and she played the last tune in the book very nicely, for she had learnt music a long time, quite four years. Pat was not at all frightened, either; but perhaps this was rather a pity, for he played a great many wrong notes without noticing that they were wrong, and this was not pleasant to listen to. However, he got to the end of the tune quicker than most people would have done, and that was enough for Pat. Elfie took twice as long as Pat over her piece, though it was a very short one, on the first page of the book. She was not shy, but she was painstaking, and when she played a wrong note she always went back and tried all the other notes within reach until she hit upon the right one, which showed great perseverance. Cousin Sylvia did not play from the book at all. She played a wonderful tune out of her head, that flew all over the piano and was full of runs and trills and most enormous chords. Sylvia had great talent for music, everybody said.

"Thank you, my dear," said Grandmamma. "I, too, had great talent for music when I was your age, although I was not allowed to use the pedals or to put so much expression into my piece as you do. It was not considered nice when I was a girl." It was very difficult to feel conceited, when Grandmamma was in the room.

THE DUET ❧ ❧ ❧ ❧

L AST of all, Pat and Elfie played a duet. They did not exactly keep together, for Pat played so much faster that he got to the end several bars ahead of Elfie, and then said: "Make haste, Elfie!" in a loud whisper, which flurried Elfie dreadfully, and made her skip some of the tune in order to catch him up. Unfortunately, she forgot to skip with both hands at the same time, so the result was rather confusing. Still, they both counted so loudly all the time that perhaps nobody heard the tune.

"They do not say we have great talent for music, Pat," said Elfie, when they had both finished.

THE END OF BABY'S
CHRISTMAS ❧ ❧

THEN something rather depressing happened. It always happens every day; but somehow, on Christmas Day, it seems worse than usual. Nurse suddenly appeared at the drawing-room door.

Baby did not seem to see Nurse. This was odd, because she certainly followed him all over the room. But whenever she came near him, Baby saw something that interested him in the opposite direction, and away he went after it. This went on for some time, till at last Nurse said: "Baby is such a good boy, he is coming to bed without any fuss."

Baby did not appreciate this compliment. "I'm not a good boy," he said. "I'm a bad boy, and I'm going to stay up a little longer."

"Oh, Baby!" said Mother. "If you are not a good boy,

Santa Claus will not bring you any toys next Christmas."

This made Baby a little sad, until he remembered what a long way off next Christmas was. "I've got my new drum now," he pointed out to Mother.

"Dear me," said Mother, "where is your new drum?"

"Upstairs," said Nurse. "Let us go upstairs and find it."

"Say good-night first," said Nancy, "in case we do not see you again."

"You will see me again," said Baby, as he kissed everybody in turn.

But he said this in a very sleepy voice, and long before he found his way upstairs to his new drum he was sound asleep in Nurse's arms. And that was the end of Baby's Christmas.

THE LAST DANCE OF THE DAY

"IN my young days," said Grandmamma, "we always finished up Christmas Day with Sir Roger."

"We always finish up that way, too," said the children, glad for once to be able to say that their days resembled the perfect days to which Grandpapa and Grandmamma were always referring.

Sir Roger is a dance for everybody's young days and for everybody's old days as well. So when Grandpapa led Grandmamma to the top of the long line of dancers, and Elfie trotted to the bottom with her youngest boy cousin, there was nothing odd-looking about it. To be sure, Elfie ran a little faster than Grandpapa, and reached the middle long before he was there to swing her round; and Grandmamma was so very stately that she nearly got left behind altogether when they danced round in procession; and it was a little difficult for Father and Mother to get through the arch made by Pat and Nancy; but these things are of no consequence on Christmas Day. Old people grow young,

and little people grow big, when Santa Claus and the fairies are about.

"I have not enjoyed a dance like that since I was a boy of twenty, and that must be five-and-fifty years ago," said Grandpapa, when he led Grandmamma to her seat after the dance.

Nancy's eyes grew round with wonder as she did a hasty sum in her head. "Only think," she whispered to Cousin Bob; "Grandpapa is a hundred and ten years old!"

Arithmetic was not Nancy's strong point; so Cousin Bob did a sum in his head, too.

"Grandpapa is only ninety-five years old," he said.

Arithmetic did not seem to be anybody's strong point, just then. But, perhaps, the fairies had something to do with that.

THE END OF THE DAY

IT is a pity that pleasant things cannot go on for ever. Even on Christmas Day, this cannot be arranged; and so, for the second time that evening, Nurse appeared at the drawing-room door. Luckily, unpleasant things can be made to turn into pleasant ones—if the fairies are about. That, no doubt, is why the rather silent little people, who went so unwillingly upstairs at the end of Christmas Day, were so full of sleepiness and drowsiness that they were quite glad to see their warm, soft beds in the night nursery. And the fairies who flew from pillow to pillow, dropping a nice dream on each, felt they had arranged everything perfectly.

Nobody had been cross, all day long. Nobody had been greedy or silly. Nobody had wanted anybody else's present. The fairies were very pleased with themselves as they flew back to Fairyland.

THE POSTMAN'S CHRISTMAS BOX

Boxing Day

WHY is it called Boxing Day?" asked Baby.

"Because it is the day we give people their Christmas boxes," said Father. "Look! There is the postman; run and give him his Christmas box."

All this was very puzzling to Baby; but he did what he was told, and stood on tiptoe and gave the postman his Christmas box. "Though it isn't a box really," he added apologetically; "it's just pennies." The postman did not mind this; he liked pennies best.

"The poor postman deserves his Christmas box," said Mother. "He has to go out in all weathers to take people their letters."

"I should like to be the poor postman," said Baby. "The poor postman can stamp in the puddles all day long."

"I expect the postman is tired of stamping in puddles," said Mother. Baby thought this highly improbable.

Presently, the waits came up for their Christmas box, too. When the children heard this, they were most excited and ran out on the door-step to see what these wonderful musicians looked like in the daylight.

"Oh!" said Elfie, in a disappointed tone. "It's only old Jo Brown."

"And Jim Potter," added Nancy. "And Tom Bunce," added Pat.

"And they haven't any instruments!" cried all the children together.

The waits had no idea they were disappointing anybody. "The best of New Years to you all," they said, beaming with smiles.

"Thank you," said Elfie, politely but sadly. "Would you please tell us why you looked so different on Christmas Eve? Was it the fairies who made you all white and shining and magical?"

The waits were extremely astonished to hear themselves described like this. "It must have been the moon, for sure," said old Jo Brown, scratching his head.

THE VILLAGE BAND

IN every village of the right kind the band always comes up to play to the Squire on Boxing Day. It does not come alone; nearly the whole village comes with it, which, of course, is only necessary. There must be someone to walk in front of the band, and someone to open the gate, and someone to hold up the music, and someone to stand about with a pipe in his mouth. That is why the Squire's garden is always quite full by the time the band has arrived in it.

"There is not very much band," said Baby, when he saw all the people who had come with the band. "I will help them with my new drum." And he did.

THE BUTCHER'S CHRISTMAS BOX

THE butcher's pony must have known it was Boxing Day, for when his master had left the meat at the back door as usual, he refused to move any way but backwards; and although a pony who walks backwards is very useful in a circus, he is a little tiresome in a back yard. However, in this case it was most fortunate that he was such a gymnastic pony; for if he had galloped straight off like any other pony, the butcher would not have been there when the children came running out with his Christmas box. But no sooner had he pocketed it, than the pony stopped behaving like a circus pony and cantered off as nicely as possible. That just shows how clever ponies are!

THE  CARRIER'S CHRISTMAS BOX

IF the door of the Hall had not stood open on Boxing Day, the door-bell would have been ringing all the morning. But the Squire never shut his door to anyone; besides, on Boxing Day, the children were all waiting to give people their Christmas boxes. When the carrier came, they had a race downstairs to see who would get to him first. Nancy won the race. "Isn't it a lovely surprise?" she cried, as she gave him his Christmas box. The carrier did not seem so much surprised as he might have been

THE BELL-RINGERS

THE bell-ringers certainly deserve a Christmas box. They have done more than anybody to remind people that Christmas is here again. It cannot be pleasant to go up into a cold dark belfry, night after night, just to ring the Christmas bells. But the bell-ringers do not grumble. Other people can only mention to those they meet that Christmas has come. The bell-ringers ring out the news to people they cannot even see. That is much better than sitting at home and talking about the nasty weather outside.

"Do you get tired of ringing bells?" asked Nancy of the head bell-ringer.

"Sometimes, missy," he answered.

"Why do you not ask the fairies to help you?" asked Elfie. "Fairies are used to ringing bells."

"I never saw no fairies in our belfry, missy," said the bell-ringer.

This surprised Elfie. "That must be because you are grown-up," she said.

BABY'S CHRISTMAS BOX

P LEASE, I want a Christmas box," said Baby.

"Those that ask don't have," said Nurse, who could always think of things like this to say at the right moment.

"I'm not asking," said Baby; "I'm only waiting."

Grandpapa gave one of his big chuckles at this. "Come and see what Grandpapa has in his pocket," he cried.

Baby hastened to accept this invitation, and he found a round pink box filled with chocolate creams in Grandpapa's pocket. This was a much better Christmas box than the postman's, thought Baby.

"People who have Christmas boxes should always give some away to other people," said Mother.

"I have only one Christmas box though," said Baby.

"Yes," said Mother; "but there are many chocolates in it."

"How many?" asked Baby. "Are there a thousand?"

"There are too many to count," said Mother.

"There are not too many to count now," said Baby sadly, when he had handed round his Christmas box.

GRANDMAMMA'S MEMORY ❧

WAS there a Boxing Day in your young days, Grandmamma?" asked Pat.

"There were many Boxing Days when I was a child," said Grandmamma. "And there has been many a one since," she added, with a little sigh.

"How many a one has there been since?" asked Nancy.

Grandmamma counted. "There were about as many as Baby has seen, from the time I left school till the time I met Grandpapa," she said, marking off her Boxing Days on her fingers, "and about as many again before I married Grandpapa; and after that—after that——"

"How many were there after that, Grandmamma?" asked Sylvia.

But Grandmamma lost count here. Perhaps it was because she had only ten fingers on her hands.

"Were there more than a hundred, do you think?" asked Elfie.

Grandmamma could not remember more than a hundred Boxing Days; and Elfie looked disappointed. "I hope I shall remember more than a hundred when I am as old as you are, Grandmamma," she said. She did not think much of Grandmamma's memory.

"In my young days," said Grandmamma, changing the conversation, "I did not have nearly so much amusement as you young people have at Christmas time. I had very few games, and very few parties, and very few presents."

"What did you have, Grandmamma?" cried Bob in amazement.

"I had my task to do every day," said Grandmamma, "and my sampler to work. And sometimes, for a treat, I went to call upon my Aunts."

"Did you not play cricket, Grandmamma?" cried Bob.

"I did nothing to make myself hot or untidy," she said.

The children were very glad they had not lived in Grandmamma's young days.

THE END OF BOXING DAY ❧

IT is very easy to feel sleepy after tea, on Boxing Day. But it is never easy to go to bed. So, first of all, Baby began to be cross; and Nurse whisked him off to bed. Then Elfie began to yawn, and she was whisked after him. Then Pat, declaring sleepily that he was wide awake, was carried off, too; and he fell asleep before he was undressed.

The older ones pretended to read story-books. But it was no use; and when Nurse found them all sitting in a row with their heads nodding, she whisked them off, too. "No nonsense for me!" said Nurse.

No one thought of contradicting Nurse when she said this.

PREPARING FOR THE SNOW-BALL FIGHT

Christmas Week

CHARLES ROBINSON.

THERE'S such a funny man in the garden, Nancy," said Elfie, in a frightened whisper. "He's all white, and he doesn't answer when you speak to him, and he's lumpy all over."

"Don't be frightened," said Nancy. "I'll take care of you." She was very glad to have hold of Elfie's hand, though, when they came to the funny man. "Let's shake hands with him," she suggested in rather a jerky voice. But when they touched the man's hand, it melted away. That sometimes happens—if you are made of snow.

THE SNOW-BALL FIGHT

THE boys were on the lawn, making snow-balls and piling them up in heaps. They were going to lie in wait for the girls and then attack them. "It will be like the Charge of Balaclava,"* said Cousin Bob, who learned history.

Unfortunately, while they were still making snow-balls, the girls suddenly sprang out from behind the bushes and attacked them instead. Then there was a terrific fight. The boys were so taken by surprise, that they could do nothing at first but duck their heads before the fire of snow-balls. They had lost all their ammunition, for Cousin Sylvia had pounced upon that directly she made the attack upon them. So the boys were very glad when Grandpapa suddenly appeared on the scene and came to their aid.

Grandpapa had not been a real General for nothing, and he soon told them what to do. So in another minute the girls were beaten back again into the bushes, and the boys had time to breathe. The girls were quite pleased with themselves, all the same.

"Wasn't it like the Charge of Balaclava?" cried Cousin Bob.

"Not a bit," said Grandpapa, who knew more history than Cousin Bob.

"How do you know, Grandpapa?" said Cousin Bob, taken aback.

"Because I was there," answered Grandpapa.

* A famous and fierce battle in the Crimean War.

CHARLES ROBINSCIN

THE BOYS ARE TAKEN BY SURPRISE

THE SLEIGH

A WHEEL-BARROW has many uses. It can hold grass, or weeds, or flowerpots, or children. It can pretend to be a ship, a train, or a motor-car. Best of all, it can be

turned into a sleigh by having its wheels taken off. When it is a sleigh, it gives occupation to a whole family, which is a great advantage in the holidays. Everybody who cannot squeeze inside can help to pull it along, which, if not quite so interesting, is certainly safer when the sleigh turns over and scatters people in the snow.

THE SLEIGH

Page 140

THE CHRISTMAS TREE

Page 153

THE SLEIGH

SLIDING ໒ঞ ໒ঞ ໒ঞ ໒ঞ

CHARLES ROBINSON

A LOVELY long slide stretched from one end of the pond to the other. Elfie could not slide well enough to keep up the whole way; but Cousin Bob came along behind her and pushed her the rest of the way, which came to the same thing in the end. "See how well I slide!" cried Elfie.

"See me, too!" cried Baby, and he sat down on the ice. This, however, was not what he had intended to do, and he felt a little upset. "I don't like this floor," he complained. "It slips away. Nasty floor!"

Nurse picked him up and carried him indoors. She did not like that kind of floor either. She preferred a nice tidy nursery, with a big fire, and no toys lying about.

ON THE ICE

SKATING ✦ ✦ ✦ ✦ ✦

THERE are many ways of skating. One way is to twirl round on one foot and declare it is quite easy. That was Cousin Sylvia's way. Another way is to push a chair along till your hands and feet nearly drop off with the cold, and you wish you had stayed indoors. That was Nancy's way. Another way is to charge wildly into everybody and tumble down every other minute. That was Pat's way. And another way is to stand on the bank and say: "Ah, this reminds me of fifty years ago!" That was Grandpapa's way.

THE TOBOGGAN ✦ ✦ ✦

PAT had a splendid idea. It was such a good idea that he thought he would keep it to himself, which, of course, was not only greedy but a little lonely and superior as well.

"Where are you going, Pat?" asked his sisters, when they saw him creeping out of the house with a tea-tray in his hand.

Pat pulled up short and looked rather foolish. "I'm going to slide down that lovely white hill over there," he said.

They did not seem to think much of his splendid idea.

"I don't want to come," said Nancy, tossing her head.

"I don't want to come," said Elfie, tossing her head.

There was altogether something very wrong with Pat's splendid idea. It did not turn out to be nearly so splendid as he had expected to find it. Who would have thought, for instance, that the harmless-looking mound of white snow at the  bottom of the hill was really a remarkably prickly holly-bush? Certainly Pat had no suspicion of such a thing until he found himself most uncomfortably placed on the top of it, without his tea-tray.

"Do you like tobogganing, Pat?" asked his sisters, when he came home again.

"I think it is greatly overrated," answered Pat.

"It was very kind of you not to ask us to go with you," said Pat's sisters when they saw Pat's bruises.

The Christmas Party

THE INVITATION

PEOPLE who are not yet eight years old do not have letters every day; so when the postman brought one to Nancy, she found it a little difficult not to be superior about it. "Anybody else got any letters to-day?" she enquired, looking round the nursery breakfast-table.

"Make haste and open it," was all Pat said to this; so Nancy stopped being superior and opened her letter.

"How lovely!" she cried, jumping up and down in her chair for joy. "How beautiful! Why are you not glad, all of you?"

Sylvia pointed out that they could not be glad until they knew what there was to be glad about, a view of the case that had not struck Nancy before. So she read her letter aloud, and this is what was in it:—

"My dear Nancy, Will you and your brothers and sister and all your cousins come to our Christmas party next Saturday? I hope you are quite well. I am quite well. It is a fine day. Your loving friend, Betty."

Then all the other people round the table jumped up and down in their chairs for joy, excepting Nurse, who asked how Nancy was going to answer the letter. This depressed Nancy a little; and she said, hastily and politely, that she thought Sylvia would do it much better. But Sylvia said, also very politely, that it was Nancy's letter, not hers. So Nancy shut herself up with the inkpot for a whole hour; and this was the result:—

"My dear Betty, We will all come to your party next Saturday. Thank you very much. Your loving friend, Nancy."

DRESSING FOR THE PARTY

ANYBODY might have thought that Nurse was going to the party herself. She began making preparations for it directly after dinner. She lighted a fire in the night nursery. She spread out everybody's best frock on the bed, and everybody's hair ribbon, and all the party slippers and the party stockings and the party gloves. Best of all, she let everybody begin dressing half an hour earlier than anybody need have done. "No helter-skelter for me," said Nurse.

The boys were not nearly so eager to get ready for the party as the girls were. They grumbled at having to come in from the garden to dress. They grumbled at having to put on stiff and starchy clean collars. They grumbled at having to wash their hands and faces at such

an odd time of day. "Why can we not go as we are?" they asked.

"No one would know it was a party, if you did," said the girls.

"It would be a much nicer party," said the boys.

"I am glad parties come but once a year," said Bob.

THE CHRISTMAS-TREE

"DID it grow up all in one night?" asked Elfie, when she saw the beautiful, shining, glistening Christmas-tree.

"It took all yesterday as well," said Betty, thinking of the dolls she had dressed and tied on the tree.

"Did it come up through the carpet slowly, or did it spring up suddenly with a bang?" asked Elfie, looking at the tree with her big round eyes.

Betty was two years older than Elfie, so she felt extremely grown-up. "Christmas-trees

don't grow like other trees," she said in a superior tone.

Elfie smiled. "I know they don't," she said. "They come from Fairyland, of course!"

THE BRAN PIE

BABY was greatly disappointed in the appearance of the bran pie. "Where's the pie-crust?" he demanded.

"Bran pies do not have any crust," explained his little hostess, as politely as she could. "Bran pies are not like other pies."

"Are they good to eat?" asked Baby, and he put a handful in his mouth to try. Unfortunately, this made Baby choke, and he made his new party suit in such a mess with the bran that he had to be carried off to be brushed. "I don't think it is a pie at all," said Baby sadly, as soon as he could speak.

Other people were not so particular as Baby about the bran pie. Other people put in their hands, and felt about in the bran, and pulled out interesting parcels. It was great fun to tear off the paper and see what was inside the parcels. Some people, like Pat, thought the biggest parcel would be the best; and then they were disappointed when they found that they had to pull off paper after paper, until they came to a tiny present in the middle, and everybody laughed at them for their pains. But other people, like Elfie, felt about for the smallest parcel, and then they pulled out a dear little dolly's hat, trimmed with flowers and ribbons, just like any grown-up lady's hat from Paris.

"See what comes of not being greedy," said Betty's nurse approvingly.

"It wasn't because I'm not greedy," Elfie explained. "It was because I thought the tiny presents would be the ones the fairies had brought."

Everybody laughed at this, except Betty's mother; and she kissed Elfie. "I hope you will always get the fairies' presents," she said.

"So do I," said Elfie.

POOR JENNY

OOR JENNY is a-weeping," sang the children, as they danced round Baby.

"I'm not weeping!" roared Baby indignantly. "I'm laughing!" And he got up from the floor and tried to escape from the ring. But when he found that this was not the game,

and that he had to stop where he was until someone came and kissed him, the corners of his mouth began to go down.

He did not like being kissed by strange little girls in party frocks.

"Poor Jenny is a-weeping!" sang the children, as Nancy carried off Baby in tears.

ORANGES AND LEMONS ⚬⚬⚬

I 'LL be oranges and you can be lemons," said Bob in a loud whisper to Betty, as they held up their hands for the procession of children to pass under. It is fortunate that a whisper is more easily heard than a shout; for otherwise poor Betty would not have had many people on her side. As it was, however, she had as many as Bob by the time that everybody's head had been chopped off except Baby's.

"Here comes the chopper to chop off your head!" they sang. "Chop, chop, chop—!"

Then down came the chopper, and Baby was asked which he would have.

"Both, please," said Baby,
looking round for the oranges
and lemons. " I don't see any

oranges," he mentioned, when he was banished to the tail of
the children behind Bob.

Then everybody pulled, and
everybody shrieked, and everybody tumbled down, and it was
impossible to say who had won.
But Baby knew fast enough.
" I've won," he announced; "and
I'm waiting for my oranges,
please."

NUTS IN MAY

THE MULBERRY-BUSH

THE great thing at a party is to avoid playing the same game too long. Betty, who was a most experienced little party lady, knew this quite well; so she chose just the right moment to turn "Oranges and Lemons" into "Nuts in May"; and, long before people were tired of "Nuts in May", she turned it into the "Mulberry-Bush". To be sure, the mulberry-bush was a Christmas-tree; but then, who has ever heard of a party that danced round a real mulberry-bush? There would be no sense in singing: "Here we go round the Mulberry-Bush", if everybody could see the mulberry-bush all the while. One would simply keep quiet about it. That is why it is quite as easy to play the Mulberry-Bush game without a mulberry-bush as it is to "wash our face" without a sponge. A real sponge would spoil the fun altogether.

GROWN-UP DANCING ❧ ❧

GROWN-UP dancing is quite different from children's dancing, and much more exciting. Betty explained that the dancing at her party was going to be the grown-up kind, and that the boys would ask the girls to dance, and the girls were not to dance with one another. Everybody was most impressed when Betty said this. The little girls sat round the room on chairs and looked important. The boys kept together in a crowd near the door and longed for supper. They whispered among themselves. They tugged at their collars and looked up at the ceiling when Betty frowned at them.

They did not show the least sign of meaning to ask anybody to dance with them.

"I think grown-up dancing is very dull," at last said Elfie in a loud tone. "Come here, Pat, and dance with me at once." Pat was very glad to come. It was draughty by the door, and he was far too shy to ask any strange little girl to dance with him.

Baby was not too shy. He marched up to the most grown-up little girl he could see, and this happened to be Betty's eldest sister, who tied her hair up with a ribbon and learned French and the violin.

"Come and dance!" said Baby. They were not a well-matched couple, but Baby felt tremendously grand every time he was whirled off his legs, which happened very often. Baby quite approved of the grown-up way of dancing. Generally he could not choose his partner, but had to dance with some-one his own size, who could not whirl him off his legs.

"Do it again!" he shouted, when the dance came to an end. But his partner did not seem to hear this second invitation to the dance.

THE CRACKERS

THE crackers at Betty's party were full of surprises. There was a fool's cap in them for Betty's eldest sister, which was an absurd present to give anyone who could speak French and play the violin. And there was a whistle in them for Pat, which was not really a useful present for anybody who already made as much noise as two people. Then there was a college cap for Bob, who, though a splendid half-back, could never learn his lessons; and there were all sorts of puzzles and fire-balloons and riddles and toys for all the others. And for everybody there was a glorious noise of big guns and explosions. Baby, unfortunately, did not like big guns and explosions.

"Take 'em away; they frighten me!" he roared.

"Oh, Baby!" said Betty's eldest sister. "I'd be ashamed. Little boys are never frightened."

"Some little boys are," shouted Baby, who did not seem at all ashamed.

FORFEITS

IT is not pleasant to be made to look foolish, but it is very good for one. Bob knew this because he had heard it said so very often; but it did not make him like it any better when he had to stand in the middle of the room, with everybody laughing at him, and bite an inch off the end of the poker. He thought it was a very stupid thing to have to do. There were some things, a chocolate-stick, for instance, that he would have had no objection to biting; but a black and smoky poker was very different. However, he could not shirk it, with all those girls giggling at him; so he opened his mouth slowly, lifted the poker, and—

"You silly boy!" laughed Betty. "Bite an inch *away* from it!"

"Now, why didn't I think of that before?" wondered Bob.

SPINNING THE TRENCHER 🌸

SPINNING the trencher* is an anxious game. You sit and sit and sit, waiting for your name to be called. You cannot take any interest in your neighbours, or hold a conversation with anybody, or enjoy a moment's happiness. You have to pretend you do not mind a bit when other people's names are called; and you say now and then, in a loud voice: "I have not been called yet," to remind the person, who is spinning the trencher, that you are waiting. You grow more and more unhappy as the game goes on, and just when you have given up hope, and are perhaps enjoying a quiet and comfortable yawn, your name is called and you do not hear it until the trencher has done spinning.

Baby did not find it an anxious game, though. He made it a little anxious for everybody else; but that was another matter. He soon grew tired of seeing other people spin the trencher; so he just got up and span it on his own account, whenever he felt inclined. And, unfortunately for the other

---

*A trencher is a large wooden serving platter.

players, he felt inclined very often.

"You must wait for your name to be called, Baby," explained Betty's eldest sister. "That is not the way to play."

"I like this way better," smiled Baby. And he bounded towards the trencher with such vigour that he knocked it over and sat on it.

"I've won!" said Baby, beating a tattoo on the trencher with his heels.

"No," said Betty; "you have not won. You have lost, and the trencher is ours."

"But I am sitting on it," Baby reminded her.

Baby certainly won, that time.

GOING HOME

GOING home is the sad part of the party. It is very difficult to keep one's eyes open. It is very hard to have no party to look forward to on the morrow. It is not easy to keep one's temper when somebody else, who forgets that the party is over, tries to be funny and tips people into the deep snow. And it is most difficult of all not to feel depressed when Nurse says, "You've all had too much party; that's what it is!"

But when the hall door flies open and shows Mother on the door-step, waiting to hear all about the party, one forgets these disagreeable things. It is only Nurse, after all, who thinks it is because we have stayed too long at the party that we are sleepy. Mothers know better.

THE PANTOMIME

TO-MORROW," said Mother, looking mysterious, "something is going to happen."

"Something nice or something nasty?" asked several voices.

"I wonder which you would call it," said Mother, thoughtfully.

But anybody could see from the look in the corner of her eye that she knew it was something people would wish to happen.

"Oh, Mother!" gasped Elfie. "Is it—is it the pantomime?"*

Mother nodded. "Cinderella," she said.

All the children screamed and danced for joy when they heard this, from superior Cousin Bob down to Baby.

"I've seen four pantomimes," said superior Cousin Bob. "I hope this one will be good."

"Hooray!" shouted Baby. "We're going to have a pantymime!"

Then he whispered to Nancy, who always knew everything and never laughed at him, "Please, is it something to eat or to drink?"

*A play in which the actors use few or no words.

[171]

THE DEMONS 𝒫 𝒫 𝒫 𝒫

THE pantomime began with the demons. "Panto-mimes always begin with demons," said superior Cousin Bob.

"Why?" asked Baby.

Cousin Bob did not know. "Listen to the pantomime," he said.

"I wish they didn't begin with demons," said Baby. "I wish they'd turn up the gas."

The pantomime people must have heard this, for the demons suddenly went down a hole, and the lights went up.

THE FAIRIES ❧ ❧ ❧ ❧

ELFIE could not believe that she was really looking into Fairyland at last. There were all the glittering fairies she had always longed to see. There was the fairy Godmother, and the fairy Queen. And they really held wands in their hands and wore stars in their hair, and were much, much more beautiful than she had ever imagined they could be.

"The fairies always bore me rather," said the cousin who had been to four pantomimes.

Elfie looked at him with big distressed eyes.

"Don't!" she whispered. "They might hear you!"

They certainly must have heard the enormous laugh that Bob gave when Elfie said this. But to her great relief they did not turn Cousin Bob into anything unpleasant.

THE FUNNY MAN

"OW, this is the part I like!" said Cousin Bob, when Cinderella's stepmother came bounding on the stage and turned a somersault.

"What a funny man!" said Nancy. "Why has he got somebody else's clothes on?"

"That's because he is the comedian," explained superior Cousin Bob.

"No, he isn't," said Pat. "He's the stepmother."

Cousin Bob almost gave up being superior. "If you had seen as many panto-mimes as I have, you would understand these things," he said.

"Should we?" said Pat, feeling much impressed.

"I understand them now," said Baby at the top of his voice.

BETWEEN THE ACTS

WHY have they pulled down the blind?" asked Baby, when the curtain fell at the end of the Prince's ball.

"It will begin again soon," said Father.

"Will it begin all over again from the beginning?" asked Elfie, who thought that anything could happen in Fairyland.

"It is easy to see that you have never been to a pantomime before," chuckled Cousin Bob.

Elfie wondered why this was so easy to see, and she tried to return the compliment.

"It is easy to see that you have been to four pantomimes, Cousin Bob," she said politely.

Father laughed very much at this; but Cousin Bob did not seem so much amused.

"Have they gone to bed behind the blind? I wish they'd wake up. I want some more!" shouted Baby, impatiently.

Immediately, the curtain went up again. Baby was very pleased with himself.

"I have woke the pantomime up," he said.

THE PANTALOON

"ISN'T he like Grandpapa?" cried Pat, when the pantaloon* shuffled on the stage. Nancy did not think this was quite polite to Grandpapa, who was such a nice old gentleman. "I think he is much more like a crossing-sweeper," she said.

"I think he is a little bit like both," said Elfie, who always tried to agree with everybody.

"Which bit of him is like me, Elfie?" asked Grandpapa.

Elfie tried to find the nicest bit of the pantaloon for Grandpapa. "I think his funny knob of hair is like you, Grandpapa," she decided. She did not remember till afterwards that Grandpapa was bald.

*The clown.

THE HARLEQUIN 〜 〜 〜

WHO is that man dressed like a cracker?" asked Nancy. "That is the harlequin," explained Mother.

"Why doesn't the clown catch hold of him when he hits him with that funny strap?" asked Pat, knowing from experience what would happen to him if he came up behind anybody with a strap.

"The clown cannot see him," said Mother. "Nobody can see him. He is invisible."

"Somebody can see him," mentioned Baby. "I can see him."

"They cannot see him on the stage," explained Mother.

"Shall we tell them when we see him coming?" asked Baby, eagerly.

"Certainly not," said Father, in a great hurry. "It would spoil the fun."

"I don't think it would spoil the fun," said Baby. "I think, perhaps, they would like to know."

Father was quite sure they would not like to know, and Cousin Bob declared that people never did these things at pantomimes; so Baby contented himself with giving Father a big dig in the back with Grandmamma's umbrella, which was about the size of a small tent.

"I'm invisible," said Baby with a smile, when Father turned round.

"That's lucky for you," said Father. And he kept hold of Grandmamma's umbrella for the rest of the afternoon.

THE COLUMBINE ✌ ✌ ✌

WHY doesn't that fairy walk on her feet properly?" wondered Pat.

"Fairies don't walk, they skim," Elfie explained. "I'm going to practise it when I get home."

"I wonder if it hurts," said Nancy.

"Oh no," said superior Cousin Bob. "They put lumps in their toes. And she isn't a fairy, she's a columbine."

"I shall put lumps in my toes too," said Elfie. "And I'm sure she is a fairy," she added to herself. If anybody could skim like that without being a fairy, thought Elfie, what was the use of Fairyland?

AFTER THE PANTOMIME

WOULD you sooner be a clown or a fairy, Grandmamma?" asked Pat, as they all whizzed home in the motor-car.

Grandmamma seemed to have some difficulty in settling this, so Pat obligingly helped her. "I think I should like you best as a fairy," he said. "You would be so useful about the house, turning mice into ponies, and all that, you know."

"I am going to be a clown when I grow up," Cousin Bob announced.

"You look rather like a silly old clown," said Sylvia.

"Hush!" said Mother. "That is not polite."

"It may not be polite," said Sylvia, "but I can't help his looks."

"You'll be a silly girl when you grow up," said Cousin Bob in return.

"I have no intention of being a boy, thank you," said Sylvia, sweetly.

"They've had too much pantomime, that's what it is," said Nurse, when they all got home.

COMING FROM THE PANTOMIME

The New Year

GOOD-BYE to another year!" said Grandpapa, as they all sat round the fire on New Year's Eve. "This makes me feel very old."

"It makes me feel old too, Grandpapa," said Elfie, out of politeness.

"I rather like growing old," said Cousin Bob. "It makes a fellow feel he is somebody."

"I don't like growing old," sighed Cousin Sylvia. "It makes me think of long dresses and hair-pins."

"Do you like growing old, Mother?" asked Nancy.

"Growing old does not matter," said Mother, "so long as we grow better at the same time."

"I am growing better," said Baby. "Aren't you, Pat?"

"Oh, no, I don't think so," said Pat, modestly. But he did not seem quite sure of this.

Then Nurse appeared in the door-way, just as she had appeared there every night of the old year that was slipping away for ever. The seasons made no difference to Nurse.

"It will be next year when we wake up in the morning, Nurse," said Elfie, hoping to gain a little time.

"But it's this year that you are going to bed," said Nurse, who was not to be caught by this sort of trick.

AULD 🐦 🐦
LANG SYNE

ELFIE sat up in bed and listened. "Hark!" she whispered. "What is that noise?"

Several heads bobbed up from several cots.

"It's people singing," said Sylvia.

"Let's go and listen," said Nancy, putting one foot out of bed. It was very easy to let the other foot follow it, and in another minute the children were all leaning over the balusters, listening to the music downstairs in the hall.

"I know what it is," said Bob. "They're singing 'Auld Lang Syne'. People always do that on New Year's Eve."

"We never do," said Pat.

"There's no reason why we should not begin now," said Bob.

"There's Nurse," said Elfie, who thought this the best of reasons.

"She's downstairs at supper," said Bob.

So the children on the top landing all joined hands in a circle, and sang "Auld Lang Syne", just as the grown-up people were doing downstairs; and the Old Year went slowly to sleep while they sang, and the New Year came nearer and nearer and nearer.

"Be off to bed with you at once, you young rascals!" called Father from downstairs.

"It's all right," said Pat, reassuringly, as they all scuttled back to bed. "That isn't Father's serious voice."

FATHER TIME

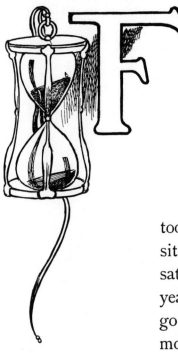

"FATHER TIME is busy to-night," said Mother, as she peeped into the night nursery on her way to the midnight service at the village church.

"Who is Father Time?" asked Elfie. "Does he live in the hall clock?"

"No," said Mother; "he is far too big to get into the hall clock. He sits up in the clouds, where he has sat for thousands and thousands of years, marking off the years as they go by; and he holds the sun and the moon in his two hands."

"What would happen if he went to sleep?" asked Nancy.

"Father Time never goes to sleep," said Mother. "He is always wide awake, and he is always watching his hour-glass. The sand is running out, grain by grain, and when the last grain has run out, the New Year has come."

"Has the last grain run out yet?" asked Pat, sleepily.

"Very nearly," said Mother.

"I will keep awake till the last grain of sand has run out," murmured Pat, as he dropped to sleep.

Father Time

TWELVE O'CLOCK

ELFIE lay awake and listened. She could hear the people going along the frosty road to church. She could hear the church bells ringing out the Old Year as fast as they could. "Poor Old Year, good-bye!" whispered Elfie.

Suddenly, the bells stopped. There was a deep and wonderful silence. Almost one could hear the last grain of sand run out of Father Time's hour-glass. Then the church clock struck twelve. The hall clock struck twelve. In the distance could be heard all the engine whistles. Every train in England was whistling in the New Year. "How do you do, little New Year?" whispered Elfie.

ON NEW YEAR'S MORNING

THE END OF  THE OLD YEAR

COUSIN SYLVIA lay awake too, as the clock struck twelve. She wondered if she had done as much as she might have done, in the year that was dying. She was certainly two inches taller, and she knew ever so many more French verbs, and she had begun German; but she did not know if these things counted.

"Bob!" she whispered. "Do French verbs count?"

But Bob only gave a snore. He had gone to sleep counting up the runs he had made at cricket in the Old Year, and he meant to do much better in the New Year. So did Sylvia. "I will try to like German," she told the little New Year.

NEW YEAR'S MORNING

"I'M a year older than I was last night, I am!" shouted Baby, as he went into the breakfast-room with the others to kiss Mother.

"So is everybody," said Father. "I have two new grey hairs."

Baby stood and looked at him carefully, when he said this. "What have you done with the old ones, Daddy?" he asked. "Did the Old Year take them away?"

"I hope so," laughed Father.

"The Old Year has not taken away your grey hairs, Grandpapa," said Baby. "Except the ones on the top," he added.

"Hush!" said Mother. "You should not say anything about people's looks, Baby. It is rude to make personal remarks."

"Come here, Baby, and let me put your hair tidy," said Nancy, to change the conversation.

"Oh, Nancy!" said Baby, in a shocked tone. "It is very rude to make personable remarks."

THE NEW CALENDAR

"WHO will put up the new Calendar?" asked Mother, bringing it into the nursery.

"I will," said Bob. "That is a man's job, that is."

"Is it because it is a man's job that you have lost the hammer twice?" teased Sylvia, at the end of five minutes. "And is it because it is a man's job that the Calendar has fallen down three times?"

"Girls always talk too much," said Bob.

"Not always," said Sylvia. And when Bob was not looking, she put up the Calendar.

"Why," said Bob, "that is just what I was going to do!"

"Well, you see," explained Sylvia, very gravely, "there are only three hundred and sixty-five days in the year, and I was afraid, if we waited till you had put up this year's Calendar, that it would be almost time to take it down again and put up next year's."

"Girls always talk too much," grumbled Bob.

NEW YEAR RESOLUTIONS

"ON New Year's Day," said Mother, "people make good resolutions for the coming year."

"And not before they're wanted," said Nurse, darkly.

"What's a resolution?" asked Baby. "Is it a game?"

"No," said Mother gravely, "it is not a game. It would be a good resolution to make up your mind to be a good boy till next year."

"I am a good boy now," objected Baby. "Mummy said so just now."

This was quite true, and it made it a little awkward for Mother. "It is always possible to be a better boy," she pointed out.

"Is it?" said Baby. He seemed depressed by this discovery.

"I know what Bob's good resolution ought to be," said Sylvia. "How about getting up in the morning?"

"How about German grammar?" retorted Bob.

"How about three helps of pudding, Pat?" said Nancy.

"How about crying 'cause the soap gets in your eyes?" retorted Pat.

Mother thought it was time to interrupt this conversation. "When I said people should make good resolutions," she said, "I meant that they should all make their own, not other people's."

Her listeners were very sorry to hear this. They thought it was much better fun to make somebody else's good resolution than to make their own.

"I shall promise the New Year not to think about the fairies in lesson-time," said Elfie. Mother looked pleased at this resolution. She kissed Elfie.

"Kiss me too!" roared Baby. "I'm going to be a better boy till next year." Mother thought this a splendid resolution, too; so she kissed Baby a great many times.

"Is next year a long way off?" asked Baby, anxiously.

"Oh, not very long," said Mother, hopefully.

Baby gave a sigh of relief. "I can be naughty again when next year comes," he said.

TWELFTH NIGHT

"NOW!" said Father, as he put the knife in the cake.

It is always a moment of great interest when anybody puts a knife into a large cake covered with pink sugar. But when it is a Twelfth-cake, and there is a bean inside, and whoever gets the bean is King or Queen for the rest of the evening, there is a very particular reason for feeling excited.

The plate of cake was passed round in solemn silence, and everybody took a piece, trying hard to play fair and not to look first to see if the bean was inside. Then they all hunted for the bean among the plums and currants; but they could not find it. "Who can have got it?" they cried.

Suddenly, Baby choked. "Nasty cake!" he grumbled. "I don't like hard bits in my cake."

"Baby has the bean!" shouted everybody. "Baby is the King!"

Baby did not seem impressed. "Nasty cake, take it away!" he said.

HANDING ROUND THE TWELFTH-CAKE

THE THAW

ELFIE stood at the nursery window, looking down into the garden. "Good-bye, little snow fairies!" she said; "good-bye!"

The snow fairies were hurrying back to Fairyland as fast as they could fly. They hurried away from some places quicker than from others, so that the green grass peeped through in great patches. On the gravel paths, the snow turned into muddy puddles, which were not at all pretty.

"The snow fairies know the Christmas holidays are over," said Elfie. "So they have gone back to Fairyland."

"You funny little girl!" laughed Cousin Bob. "Why, it is only a thaw!" Cousin Bob could not see the fairies.

GOOD-BYE

"ELL, well," said Grandpapa, "all good things must come to an end."

"Must they, Grandpapa?" said Pat. "I should like them to go on for ever."

"Then you would get tired of them," said Grandpapa.

"I get much more tired of nasty things," said Pat.

The door-step was so full, there was hardly room to move. Grandpapa and Grandmamma and all the cousins were there with their hats on; and Father and Mother and the children and Nurse were there without their hats. The motor-car snorted and puffed as if it were in a great hurry to be off; but nobody else was in a hurry.

"Come again next Christmas!" said the children.

"Ah," said Grandmamma, mysteriously, "we shall meet long before that."

"Where shall we meet, Grandmamma?" asked Nancy.

"When the summer comes," said Grandmamma, "you are all coming to stay with Grandpapa and me at the sea-side."

Then the door-step was filled with people who jumped and

skipped and danced. The good-byes were forgotten, the ugly black thaw was forgotten, everything unpleasant was forgotten. And Elfie stood with a smile on her face, thinking of a glittering green-and-blue sea, covered with glittering green-and-blue sea-fairies, all playing in the summer sunshine. "I am glad that Christmas cannot go on for ever," said little Elfie.

Here the motor-car gave a bigger snort than usual, to show that it could not possibly wait another minute; so everybody kissed everybody else, and Grandpapa and Grandmamma and all the cousins were packed inside and covered up with warm rugs, and off went the visitors down the drive and away.

"I wish it could begin all over again!" sighed Nancy.

"Come back again, Father Christmas, I want you!" shouted Baby.

"It is silly to want impossibilities," said Nurse, as she carried Baby indoors.

Father Christmas did not come back again. He must have agreed with Nurse.